I0823540

THE GUN BRANDERS

Also by William Colt MacDonald and available from Center Point Large Print:

Ghost-Town Gold
Peaceful Jenkins
Mascarada Pass
Showdown Trail
Guns Between Suns
Law and Order, Unlimited

THE GUN BRANDERS

William Colt MacDonald

Center Point Large Print
Thorndike, Maine

This Center Point Large Print edition
is published in the year 2024 by arrangement with
Golden West Inc.

First US edition: The Berkley Publishing Corp.

The text of this Large Print edition is unabridged.
In other aspects, this book may vary
from the original edition.
Printed in the United States of America
on permanent paper sourced using
environmentally responsible foresting methods.
Set in 16-point Times New Roman type.

ISBN: 979-8-89164-337-6

The Library of Congress has cataloged this record
under Library of Congress Control Number: 2024941079

I

The three riders jerked their ponies to an abrupt halt at the distant booming of the heavy guns. All three strained their ears for further sounds, but silence once more descended. Far below the bluff on which the riders sat their ponies, a man burst hastily from the clump of chaparral, already dim in the hazy depths of the canyon. A second followed the first. The two sprinted to horses, clambered into saddles and quickly disappeared around the corner of the first bend in the gulch. Neither of them had noticed the three riders sitting motionless, high above their heads.

The tallest of the trio at the edge of the bluff spoke first. "I don't know, pards, but it sure looks like a mite of skulduggery was afoot down in this canyon."

One of the others replied, "Those two hombres were sure drifting off some hasty."

And the third put in, "It's my hunch, Tucson, there's a corpse down in that chaparral. Maybe more than one. And I'd guess it was a case of murder. What do you think, Stony?"

The second rider laughed. "Old sleuth on the trail, eh, Lullaby? Won't you never forget that deputy training of yours? At that, I'm inclined to think you've called the turn."

"Right," Tucson Smith nodded. "I think I can follow Lullaby's line of reasoning. Lullaby figures if it wasn't murder, those two hombres wouldn't have sloped off so fast. If there'd been a fair fight, they'd have taken their time. And we didn't hear any more shots, once those two had commenced running, so whoever was left behind down in that brush had quit fighting. And those two faded off fast so they wouldn't get caught."

The three had taken advantage of the halt to produce Durham and cigarette papers. Tucson Smith, the biggest man of the trio, was a lean rangy individual with brick-red hair, humorous gray eyes, and a thin hooked-nose. His mouth was straight-lipped with a tiny up-curve at each corner; his jaw was muscular, determined. There was something stern and hard and at the same time kindly in Tucson's bronzed features.

Stony Brooke was somewhat shorter than Tucson, blond-complexioned with blue eyes, snub-nosed and had a good-natured smile. He was solidly built with a keg-like torso, though surprisingly light and wiry on his feet in a fracas.

The third man, Lullaby Joslin, was tall, lanky, with bony wrists. He was soft-spoken, sleepy-appearing, with lazy movements. His hair was black as an Indian's, his dark skin burned to the consistency of worn leather. His worn Levi's fit him sloppily, his boots were scuffed, his sombrero battered. The other two also were dressed in cowpuncher togs, with six-shooters hanging in holsters at their sides.

Along the Border, this trio had been known by many names—The Three Jacks, The Mesquite Musketeers and others. Perhaps, The Three Mesquiteers—riders of the mesquite country—fitted them best: they were, like the famed trio of the immortal Dumas, "one for all and all for one." But regardless of what they were called, they were the most loved and at the same time the most feared three in the southwestern cow-country. Lawbreakers hated them with a hate born of fear; those who knew them well swore they were the fastest shooting and squarest men to be found, from the Canadian line to the Rio Grande.

There was no particular reason for the Mesquiteers being in this section of the border country, except their love of excitement. They wandered through the cattle country, working only long enough at various ranches to acquire a stake with which to travel someplace else. At the present moment they weren't seeking a job, but just wandering, rather aimlessly, hoping to find some excitement. Now the shots from the canyon below, and the sight of the two hastily fleeing men, indicated they were probably on the right track.

Tucson ground out his cigarette butt on his saddle horn. "What say we drift down to the bottom of this canyon and take a look?"

Lullaby and Stony nodded. The three kicked their ponies in the ribs and traveled on, along the edge of the bluff, seeking a way down. Fifteen minutes passed before they reached a well-worn trail leading to the bottom of the deep ravine. The way was steep and uncertain, at spots cluttered with loose rock, the going a bit perilous. Eventually they reached bottom.

Here a narrow stream of clear water twisted a swift course between precipitous cliffs. Following the stream they found the canyon widening, and a short time later reached the clump of chaparral above which they'd waited an hour or so before. Followed by Stony and Lullaby, Tucson directed his mount through the mesquite and other thorny brush. A few moments later, he stopped, gazing down on the dead body of a man.

The three halted, dismounting. Without a word they spread out in different directions, scrutinizing the earth for "sign." None of them came near the body, until he had circled the earth about the silent form. Tethered back in the brush a short distance, they saw a horse, evidently the pony of the dead man. It bore on its left front shoulder a small branded wagon wheel design.

Some distance from the point at which the dead man lay, Tucson Smith dropped to one knee, bending his gaze on certain prints in the sandy soil. He stooped farther and from the trampled earth picked up a small object which proved to be the lower lift from a riding-boot heel. Then he searched the adjoining territory.

Within a few minutes, Stony and Lullaby had also inspected the ground covered by Tucson. Gradually the three approached closer, until they were standing directly above the body of the dead man.

The body was sprawled on its back. The dead man had been probably around forty-eight years old. His hair was gray and he was clothed in typical cow-country apparel. The brown sombrero had rolled from his head and lay at one side. A Colt's forty-five six-shooter was near the lifeless hand. A scarlet stain seeped into the shirt across the breast. Strangest of all, across the dead man's forehead was an ugly diagonal jagged slash and blood congealed about the wound.

Tucson knelt by the still form and examined the gun. Replacing it, he turned the corpse on its face. An ugly black hole, just under the left shoulder showed a shot in the back. Tucson looked at his companions. Both nodded, then he rolled the corpse back to its former position. Slowly he got to his feet.

"It's murder, of course. I'll tell my story," he said quietly, "and see if your deductions tally."

Lullaby and Stony agreed. Tucson continued, "Back in the brush there's the droppings of two horses which had stood close together. Farther, beyond that mesquite thicket, a third horse is waiting. Here's how it looks to me. This dead man came down here and met a second man. A third hombre was hid back in the brush. While this dead man was talking to Man No. 2, Man No. 3 dry-gulched him from ambush. The murdered man, even as he was falling, reached for his hardware and yanked it, but Man No. 2 plugged him from in front to prevent him from pulling trigger. Then Men Nos. 2 and 3, dragged their freight fast—as we saw 'em—leaving the dead man to be found by anybody that came along."

Lullaby and Stony nodded. "My idea to a gnat's ear," Stony agreed, "except—"

"I'm wondering about that bloody slash across this dead man's forehead," Lullaby cut in, voicing Stony's thought.

"That puzzles me, too," Tucson said grimly. "I see no reason for it unless one of those murdering coyotes did it in a fit of temper."

"Doesn't look like a knife slash," Lullaby offered.

Tucson said, "Something duller than a knife made that cut. One time I saw a feller who'd been cut with a gunsight. It made a gash a lot like this."

Stony scowled. "Cripes A'mighty! I see no reason for slashing up a man's forehead like this, though. The slugs in his body finished him off pretty fast—or I'm no judge of gun-wounds."

"I knew a man once who sharpened the gunsight on his forty-five," Tucson remembered. "It made a right bad weapon when he slashed at a feller. I don't know the reason for this wound, but aces to tens it was done by a gunsight."

Lullaby swore softly. "Damn a skunk that'll cut up an enemy this way. I don't know what the argument was about, but I'd say this dead man was in the right. I'd be in a mood to take up his fight, if we could find any clues to show the murderers' identity."

"This could maybe provide a clue," Tucson said. He extended the small bit of leather, with nails still sticking in it. "I found this heel-lift over near the brush where the dry-gulching coyote was hidden. I imagine it dropped off as he stepped from cover, after he'd fired."

Lullaby and Stony examined the heel-lift. Stony said, "This bit of nailed hide is off a regulation cowhand's boot, considerable worn and run over. Now if we can find the hombre who lost it, maybe we'll get some place." He handed back the bit of leather. "What do we do now, take this body to the nearest town?"

Tucson shook his head. "I don't reckon so. We'd best leave it as is, and let the sheriff come after it. Maybe a coroner will come along with the sheriff."

"How do you know there'll be a sheriff at the next town we strike?" Stony asked.

"I'm pretty sure," Tucson replied. "You'll remember that feller in Kiote City said that we were on our way to Manzanita. Manzanita is supposed to be the county seat. It should be a fair-sized town with all the authority fixings."

"I also remember," Lullaby Joslin put in, "that that same man in Kiote City told us that Manzanita was one hard burg, that was practically run by some hombre named Nervy, or some such name."

"Nirvan—Matt Nirvan," Tucson corrected.

Stony looked interested. "Manzanita—a hard town. Maybe we'll find some real excitement."

"Just hate a fight, don't you?" Lullaby drawled sarcastically.

Tucson chuckled. "Yeah, just like cow horse hates oats. If this Nirvan proves out to be what I heard about him, Stony may get more scrapping than he wants."

"You two got a lot of nerve picking on me," Stony protested. "It seems I'm always saving your hides when you hit something you couldn't handle. How about that time in Nuevo Laredo? How about Puma City? How about Verde Wells? How about—?"

"How about Manzanita?" Tucson interrupted. "That's what I'm wondering about. It may prove as tame as a sheared sheep."

"Somehow, I doubt that," from Lullaby. "We get within a few miles of the place and run into a murder. I've a sad feeling my normal rest is due to be disturbed, if you two nosy hombres decide to investigate the derelictions of one Matt Nirvan. It never pays to buck a man who runs a town to suit his own ideas." He drew a deep sigh. "But lead on. I'll trail along and hope it won't be too much work to get you out of such trouble as you get into."

"It's a shame to disturb your peace, Lullaby," Tucson said dryly, "but we've got to give notice of finding this body, and if that leads to a fracas, we'll have to blame it on Fate. As I remember the directions we had, we follow a trail that leads along this creek, which should be the Alamos River, seeing it cuts through these Labajada Mountains. Well, let's drift."

After covering the body of the dead man with some dry brush and loose branches, they mounted their horses and followed the twisting trail bordering the sandy banks of the river. Gradually, both stream and canyon widened, the rock bluffs on either side became lower. In time the riders found themselves riding through the Labajada foothills. By now the sun had reached the meridian and they emerged into rolling grass country. Still following the river trail, which ran all the way to Manzanita, the three men crossed the water at a point where the river forked, and started climbing a long gradual slope.

"That small fork," Tucson remembered, "is known as Cottonwood Creek, according to what that man in Kiote City told me."

"Nice clear-looking stream," Lullaby observed, glancing back at the fork which ran directly south.

The fork was left behind. The riders began to pass small bunches of Herefords bearing the Wagon-Wheel brand. It was close to two in the afternoon when the three topped a rise and caught their first view of Manzanita. The town was still seven or eight miles distant, but now the going was all downhill along a well-rutted wagon trail.

Tucson touched spurs to his horse. "C'mon, pards," he called, "let's get going. My stomach is mighty empty, and we'll have to find the sheriff before we can eat."

The three raced down the slope, side by side, each wondering if some sort of trouble lay ahead, and each feeling certain in his bones that it did.

II

Manzanita, being the seat of Manzanita County, boasted a population of some seven hundred people—both good and bad—including a large number of half-breed Indians and Mexicans, these two latter types being far more peacefully inclined than a goodly portion of the so-called Anglos who'd been steadily drifting in over the past several years. The town consisted of a number of saloons, two general stores, a frame courthouse and various other places of commercial enterprise. Most of the buildings were of adobe structure. The main street was unpaved; the walks on either side were dirt paths or occasional stretches of planks. There was an almost unbroken line of hitchracks on each side, and a number of wagons and ponies were spaced unevenly, the ponies standing droop-tailed and heads down beneath the broiling heat of the afternoon.

Tucson Smith and his two companions slowed pace as they entered the town, stopping first at a small general store. Here they dismounted and entered to purchase cartridges. Outside, beneath the overhang of wooden awning, they paused a moment to fill depleted loops in their cartridge belts. Lullaby asked, "What's our first move, Tucson?"

"Find the sheriff and tell him about the dead man we found." Tucson pointed along the street, past a number of pedestrians that moved on the walks. "I can see a sign that says 'Sheriff's Office.' C'mon, we'll drift across."

He and Stony started. Lullaby hesitated, "Hey, you two, aren't we going to fork our broncs?"

Stony grinned. "You lazy, sheepherding mule! Do you mean to say you can't walk that distance?"

Tucson pointed again to the sheriff's sign. "There's the law's hangout, Lullaby, right near the center of the town. It won't be a minute's walk."

Languidly, Lullaby waved a protesting hand. "I see your sign, sure," he yawned, "but to a man of my disposition, that's quite a spell off. I was raised in a cayuse hull, and my feet never did get used to walking."

"You mean," Tucson said, "that you never feel natural unless you've got your feet even with your head—stretched out, taking it easy. C'mon, damn your lazy hide."

Reluctantly, Lullaby joined his companions. It was less than two minutes' walk to the sheriff's office which proved to be a blocklike structure of adobe, with a wide-open door and two windows raised halfway to the top. From the edge of the wooden awning, reaching from the roof of the sheriff's office to uprights at the roadside, swung a paint-faded sign reading: Sheriff's Office. To the right of the open doorway was a smaller plaque, reading: B. F. Yarrow, Sheriff (and beneath) Trent Volpone, Deputy-Sheriff.

Crossing the small porch that fronted the building, Tucson glanced within the office. The place was empty save for a couple of cots, three chairs and a rolltop desk, on the top of which was an oil lamp with one side of its chimney smoked. A couple of calendars from meatpackers decorated the walls, and on one surface a number of fly-specked "wanted bills" occupied space.

"Looks like," Stony commented, "Sheriff Yarrow and his brother officer are absent."

"We'll separate," Tucson proposed. "It's a ten-to-one shot that the sheriff and his deputy are either out on some trail or softening the heat of the afternoon in some grog shop. We'll try the saloons first. Any law officer that goes off and leaves his office wide open this way is the type that is usually found resting one foot on a brass rail and his elbow alternating between polishing the mahogany and exercising with a bottle. So, like I say, we'll start searching and the first one to find a lawman can tell the story. Then we'll go find some chow."

They separated. Stony crossed the street, Lullaby picked out a shady side street. Tucson continued in the direction in which they'd started. He'd not progressed far when he caught sight of a pair of swinging doors, from behind which came the sound of voices and the clinking of bottles against glasses. The faded sign above the doorway proclaimed the place to be the "Brown Bottle Saloon." Tucson paused and pushed through the entrance.

The interior of the saloon was low-ceilinged and dim after the bright sun glare of the street. The bar stretched almost the width of the back wall. Two round-topped wooden tables and some straight-backed chairs were scattered about. There were about a dozen men ranged along the bar which was presided over by a wizened individual with thinning hair, a chirpy voice and a quick energetic manner.

Tucson's spurs clanked across the floor and he found a vacant spot at the bar. The bartender chirped, "What'll it be, stranger?"

"A small bourbon with a lot of water to tail it."

The drink was set out and Tucson spun a silver dollar on the bar. The barkeep pushed back the money. Tucson glanced at it. His gaze went to the barkeep's smiling features. "That's good money," Tucson stated.

"I don't doubt it, cowboy." The man nodded genially. "But you can't spend it on your first drink in my place. That's my custom. Strangers never have to pay for their *first* drink. After that, they pay plenty." His smile broadened.

Tucson found himself liking the little man.

"That's fine. But I want to pay for my drink. Maybe we'd best have another. A man doesn't need a college education to appreciate the stuff you pour. That's good bourbon."

"None better in town," the other said promptly. "Not even that served in the Purgatoire. I'm proud of that fact, stranger."

"Never heard of the Purgatoire."

The barkeep lowered his voice a trifle and glanced along the counter. "You'll hear of it—plenty—if you stay in Manzanita. Matt Nirvan's place. Well, if you're buying a drink, I'd better get busy." He stretched out one hand. "I'm Johnny Jempep—better known as Johnny Jump-Up, proprietor and sole owner of the Brown Bottle, in business for twenty years, from the time Manzanita was just a wide spot in an old cattle trail."

"Glad to know you. My name's Smith—Tucson Smith."

They shook hands. Johnny Jump-Up's grin widened. "I warned you you'd pay plenty after your first free drink." He raised his voice to carry along the bar, "Name your shots, gents. This here is Tucson Smith who insists on buying."

The men along the bar straightened up, nodded their thanks to Tucson and gave orders. For a few minutes, only the sounds of gulping and the clinking of glasses was heard. The drinks consumed, Johnny gave the names of the other men along the bar. Some of the names escaped

Tucson, but he remembered four in particular: Sheriff “Beef” Yarrow, Deputy Trent Volpone, Squint Venner and Dobie Wonch. All were dressed in clothing typical of the cow country. The two law men wore badges.

Johnny announced that the Brown Bottle would buy a drink. This time, Tucson took a cigar. While the others were drinking he lighted up and looked them over. Sheriff B. F. “Beef” Yarrow was well named. He was pot-bellied, of medium height, dressed in corduroy pants and woolen shirt. A six-shooter hung at his side. He had a bulbous nose crisscrossed with tiny broken veins. The remainder of his features were a mottled crimson. His eyes were small, bloodshot; his manner, blustering.

Volpone, his deputy, looked more dangerous. He had surly features, a lantern jaw and pale blue eyes. His shoulders were stooped and his right hand seemed to hover perpetually above his ivory-butted Colt gun. The remaining two men were a pair, apparently poured from the same mold: ill-featured, low-browed, unshaven; tobacco-brown dribbles at mouth corners. Each wore a single gun. Tucson noted that Venner moved with a slight limp, as though one leg were shorter than the other.

Johnny Jump-Up swept away the empty glasses and commenced to wipe the bar with a damp towel. That done, he started to shine the back-bar mirror and wash glasses. Tucson moved down the bar toward the sheriff, just as Yarrow pushed aside his empty glass. Yarrow turned to face him. "You aiming to linger in Manzanita, cowboy?" he inquired, wiping his thick lips with the back of one hairy hand.

"I've not seen anything yet to make me stay," Tucson evaded pleasantly. "Matter of fact, sheriff, I came here to see you. Didn't find you in your office, so came here looking for you."

Yarrow tensed a trifle. "What you want to see me for?"

"I want to report a murder."

"Murder?" Yarrow frowned, as the word ran from lip to lip along the bar. "Who's been murdered? Where's the body?" The others pressed closer to hear Tucson.

"I don't know who the man is," Tucson said. "I left the body laying in a clump of chaparral near the Alamos River, in that canyon about fifteen miles beyond Cottonwood Creek. He'd been shot twice." Tucson continued, giving details, but leaving out any mention that he had been accompanied by Stony and Lullaby. Neither did he mention finding the bit of leather heel-lift, or say anything of seeing the two murderers hastily leave the scene of the killing.

". . . and in addition to the wounds I've told you about," Tucson concluded, "the murdered man had been slashed across the forehead with some sort of weapon. I don't understand why—" He paused, suddenly conscious of exclamations from a couple of men.

Johnny Jump-Up asked, "Did that slash look like it might have been made with a gunsight?"

Tucson nodded. "That was my guess."

"Mine too," Johnny said triumphantly. He glanced around. "What have I been telling you hombres?"

"Never mind that," Yarrow interrupted gruffly. "I want to know what—"

"It's about time we did mind such things," Johnny stated defiantly. "That ain't the first man that's been found marked that way. I figure, Beef, it's about time you dug the murderin' skunk out of his hole—or maybe there's more than one skunk."

Yarrow glared at the little man. "You mentioning any names, Johnny?"

The barkeep stiffened. "That's your job, Beef. Not mine. It's up to you to find the killer."

"C'rect," Yarrow rumbled. "You just 'tend your job, Johnny, and I'll 'tend to mine. And don't be too hasty passing out judgments. With strangers ridin' through Manzanita every day or so, I can't keep track of everybody. I'm as concerned as anybody else about these killings. I wish I could learn who's responsible." He looked meaningly at Tucson.

"You accusing me of knowing?" Tucson asked quietly.

"I'm suspecting everybody until they've been proved innocent," Yarrow boomed pompously. "If you can't prove your innocence, Smith, you're in for trouble."

Tucson laughed scornfully. "You'll have one hell of a time pinning that murder on me, sheriff."

"That may come later," Yarrow glowered. "We don't know anything about you—"

"Common sense," Tucson snapped, "should tell you I wouldn't be here reporting that murder, if I'd committed it."

"That's whatever. How do you know it's murder, in the first place? The hombre might have been killed in a square fight."

"Not with a shot in the man's back," Tucson stated. "Not with two riders getting away as fast as they could fan it, right after the shots were fired."

"What's that, what's that?" Yarrow demanded. "You didn't tell me about them two. Who were they?"

Volpone had stepped nearer the sheriff. Squint Venner and Dobie Wonch exchanged uneasy glances. Tucson leaned carelessly back, elbows resting on bar, facing the sheriff. "I'm not acquainted around here, sheriff," he said quietly, "so I don't know who the two riders were. Anyway, they were too far distant to be recognized." Tucson wasn't missing the fact that Yarrow and his deputy seemed to breathe easier, as did

Wonch and Venner. He added, "I wouldn't have wasted time telling you, Yarrow, if I'd known who the coyotes were."

The sheriff changed the subject. "Why didn't you bring the body in with you? You didn't use your head much."

Tucson smiled thinly. "Any responsible sheriff would want the body and the earth around it undisturbed, until he could go out and look things over for himself. That's why I left the murdered man and his horse, just as I found 'em."

Yarrow glared. "You hinting I ain't responsible?"

"No, I'm not *hinting*. But I'll be glad to withhold judgment until I see what action you take. In your place I know what I'd do."

"Yeah? The same being, Smith?"

Tucson produced from his pocket the bit of nail-pierced heel-lift. "Here's a chunk of leather that dropped from one of the murderer's boots. I found this not far from the body. If I were you or your deputy, I'd sort of sashay around town and inspect hombres' boots. You might uncover something."

An abrupt silence fell on the Brown Bottle. Necks craned to see the leather clue. Squint Venner finally broke the silence, "Well, catching criminals ain't in my line. Reckon I'll drift out and leave such matters to our sheriff. Comin', Dobie?"

Dobie Wonch nodded. "Yeah. No use of us staying here any longer, Squint."

The two men had nodded to the others and started toward the doorway, when Tucson straightened from his lounging position against the bar. "Just a minute, you two. Don't you think you ought to let the sheriff have a look at your boots, first?"

"Hell, no." Venner looked surprised. "Why should we? Beef knows us. We're not killers."

"That's right, Smith," Yarrow said quickly. "I know both of these boys. I can look at their boots later, if they've got business someplace else, right now. Smith, let me have that heel-lift."

Again Venner and Wonch started for the street. "Hold it, Venner," Tucson said sharply. "If your boot heels are all right, you can afford to wait."

"Now, look here, Smith—" Volpone cut in angrily.

"I'm doing plenty of looking," Tucson snapped. "There's murder been committed and two murderers might get away."

"Smith is right there," Johnny Jump-Up put in. Others in the saloon voiced similar remarks. Yarrow and Volpone could do nothing but surrender to majority opinion. Still, Yarrow tried to sidetrack Tucson, asking, "Why you so anxious to find the killer? The dead hombre a friend of yours?"

"Never saw him before," Tucson stated, "but

when it takes two skunks to down one man with a shot in the back, I'm taking sides. Until the dead man's friends come into the fight, or ask me to stay out, I'm not changing my opinion any."

"All right, all right," Yarrow conceded. "No need you gettin' proddy, Smith. We'll start looking at boots. Commencing with yours. I'll get to Venner and Wonch later."

"Are you forgetting they were in a hurry," Tucson said mockingly, "and you didn't want to detain them, sheriff?" He began to lose patience. "I'm suggesting you look at Venner's boots first. I've already noticed his heels aren't even."

Venner swallowed hard. "You—you accusing me of this murder, Smith?"

Tucson nodded. "Until you've proved yourself innocent. Both you and Wonch. You're about the same build as the two hombres that took off fast."

Venner and Wonch had spread out a trifle. Wonch hastily whispered something to Venner. Tucson couldn't catch the words. Wonch stepped forward. "I ain't afraid to have my boots examined," he sneered. "Here you are, Smith"—lifting one foot.

Tucson shook his head. "I reckon that's the sheriff's job."

"Go ahead, Smith," Yarrow gave surly permission.

Wonch moved nearer, and again lifted his foot. Venner backed a step. Tucson stooped down, his left hand reaching toward Wonch's foot. At the same moment he whirled, drawing his gun, and covered Venner, who was just reaching toward his holster.

"Don't try it, Venner," Tucson snapped. He gave Wonch's ankle a sudden twist and Wonch went tumbling to the floor, his already drawn gun spilling from his hand as he went down.

Venner, face pale, had backed off, lifting his hands in air. Tucson straightened and retreated to the bar, his drawn forty-five covering the two men. Wonch, cursing, climbed to his feet, his arms also going above his head.

"I think, sheriff," Tucson said coolly, "you'd better examine Venner's boots yourself. He and his pard don't seem to like the way I do it. In fact, as you can see, they were about to stop me doing anything more at all."

Many men in the saloon were directing looks of anger at Venner and Wonch, one of them saying, "It looks like it's up to you, Beef."

Before the sheriff could take action of any sort, Trent Volpone's voice intruded. "Smith, you drop that hawg-laig *pronto,* or it will be the worse for you!" The deputy's gun was leveled at Tucson.

III

There was nothing else to do, apparently. Tucson twisted around and placed his six-shooter on the bar, then lifted his arms in the air and clasped his fingers atop his sombrero. "Just what's the idea, deputy?" he asked coldly. "Every man in this barroom saw those two starting to draw on me, even while I was supposed to be looking at Wonch's boot."

"You'll find out soon enough," Volpone snapped. "Beef and I don't intend to let strange cowpokes come to town and start trouble."

The sheriff added a pompous, "By Gawd, that's right, Trent. Lawlessness has got to stop." He swooped down on the bit of heel leather Tucson had dropped when he pulled his gun. "We'll just place you in a cell, Smith, and fit this heel to your boot when we get you there."

"I don't doubt you could," Tucson stated, "after you'd worked on one of my boots and that heel a mite. It would make a neat little frame-up." He appealed to the others in the saloon. "Does this fat-headed sheriff often get away with this sort of business?"

No one answered, except Johnny Jump-Up who said, "Beef, why not try fitting that heel to Venner's boot and see if Smith has called the turn?" No one backed up that suggestion. Completely cowed, but recovering their nerve, Venner and Wonch stood at one side, looking anxious to again get their guns in hands, but not quite daring to risk it.

Yarrow growled, "I'm handling this case. There's more important matters than fitting heels, the same being to toss Smith in a cell and find out *all* he knows about this murder."

"It wouldn't hurt to try that heel on Venner's boot," Johnny Jump-Up persisted. "It was plain as day what those two intended. I saw it and so did everybody else—"

"You, Johnny,"—Yarrow sounded infuriated—"see too gawddam much. One of these days you won't be seeing nothing a-tall, if you push your face in where it ain't wanted. And now I'm putting Smith under arrest. I hope nobody shows any objections."

Johnny went white, but said something about not liking the deal Smith was getting. Volpone sneered, "Nobody's going to object, Beef. C'mon, we'll take the bastard to a cell—"

"Where were you intending to go?" came a soft drawl from the doorway.

Everyone in the barroom swung toward the door. There, just within the swinging doors, stood Stony Brooke, a broad smile creasing his round face. His six-shooter was spinning, one finger through trigger guard, in his right hand, the butt landing with a resounding *plop!* in his palm, at each revolution of the gun. *"Uh-huh!"* his head moving from side to side. "I don't figure to let you take Tucson any place."

Tucson laughed softly. Volpone emitted a snarled curse. Yarrow blurted, "What the hell!"

Tucson got his six-shooter from the bar top, saying, "Glad to see you, Stony."

"Figured I might be welcome," Stony nodded, then, "Naughty, naughty, don't touch!" he warned as Yarrow's and Volpone's hands strayed toward holsters. The revolving gun had abruptly come to a stop in his fist, its muzzle covering the room. "Maybe all you hombres had best move back toward the bar where I can watch you. I don't like to be crowded none." He moved a few steps farther into the saloon as the others backed off.

Tucson chuckled, "You got here just in time, Stony. This blank ca'tridge of a sheriff was set to take me to the hoosegow."

"T'hell he was! What for?"

"Well, you see—" Tucson commenced, then abruptly paused, as a new voice spoke from beyond Stony:

"I'm seeing plenty, but I'm not understanding," said the newcomer. "Both you strangers put your guns away mighty *pronto*, or you're going to be sorry."

Events were clicking off almost too fast for the occupants of the Brown Bottle to follow.

Johnny Jump-Up gasped. Again, the tables were turned. Stony and Tucson swiftly holstered their weapons, turning to see who had given the order.

The newcomer cradled a long-barreled six-shooter in his right fist, its muzzle traveling from side to side to cover Tucson and Stony. He was a rather strange-looking individual with a pasty white face, deeply lined from dissipation. He was dressed all in black—black stiff-brim Stetson, black trousers, black boots. His shirt was of black silk. He was long-jawed, with black eyes which had a greenish cast in them. There was something baleful, evil, about those eyes.

Despite his pasty complexion the man appeared in good condition. He moved with an easy manner, almost effortless. His shoulders were wide and he was above average height with abnormally long arms.

"Matt!" Yarrow cried. "Matt Nirvan! Thank Gawd you got here—"

"Better thank me instead," Nirvan said coldly. "What's going on here? You and Volpone aren't showing up so well as law officers. And what's wrong with Wonch and Venner? They look scared to death."

"They had a little trouble," Volpone put in sullenly. Both he and Yarrow appeared to be in fear of Nirvan.

"Hell," Nirvan stated, "I could see they weren't celebrating Christmas. It looks like a lot of you boys had had some trouble. C'mon, out with it, Yarrow."

Yarrow nervously took up the story, concluding, "And this hombre, calling himself Tucson Smith, tried to make trouble, when I suspected him of doing the killing. He knocked Wonch down and threw his gun on Venner—"

"You're a liar by the clock," Tucson said quietly.

"And if Tucson says you're a liar," Stony put in, "he's correct, only maybe he was too polite to put 'damn' in front of 'liar.' "

"You two keep your mouths shut," Nirvan said coldly. "I haven't asked you to talk—"

"You're asking for a hell of a lot of trouble though," Tucson interrupted. "Look here, Nirvan, my pard and I are strangers here. You don't know us. You do know your sheriff and deputy. However, I'm still stating they're all wrong. Let Johnny, here, tell the story just as it happened."

"I'll tell it," Johnny said quietly. "Matt, these two strangers haven't had a square deal, especially Smith. Now here is what took place . . ." From that point he related the story in detail from the moment Tucson first stepped into the Brown Bottle. All the time he talked, Matt Nirvan kept his baleful eyes fastened on Stony and Tucson. His gun continued to cover the two. As Johnny concluded the story, Beef Yarrow burst out:

"Don't you believe it, Matt. Jump-Up has got

things all twisted. He's got his facts mixed."

"Like hell he has," Tucson stated. "I still want to see if that boot-lift fits Venner's—"

"Forget that so-called murder for a minute," Nirvan interrupted coldly. His eyes bored into Tucson's and Stony's. "There's too many strangers drifting around Manzanita lately. I'm figuring to make this a town of law and order, and I know how to handle drifters. You've tried to make the sheriff and his deputy look bad, and humiliated two of the town's prominent citizens—"

Johnny snickered. "Prominent citizens!"

"That's enough from you, Johnny," Nirvan snapped. "You've been trying to buck me for a long time. I've heard you've warned men not to enter my place. It's hombres like you that attract the undesirable element to Manzanita."

Tucson snapped, "A decent sheriff and deputy could take care of any undesirable element that comes here, Nirvan. It looks to me as though you had more say, hereabouts, than Yarrow. If that is so, you'd best give Yarrow his orders to look into this murder business, instead of trying to shut me up. I'm demanding that you try that heel-lift on Venner's boot—"

"*You're* demanding?" Nirvan sneered. "Smith, men don't 'demand' when they talk to Matt Nirvan. Manzanita is my town, see? I run it as I see fit, and I'm doing a good job if I do say it myself. Gradually we're getting rid of the bad characters, and while I know I've made many enemies, I'll make this town clean, or die in the attempt."

"Meaning that you'll clean the town?" Stony snapped.

"I'll—" Nirvan paused, a touch of red coming to his pasty cheeks. He swung on Yarrow. "Beef, you and your deputy march these two nosy cowpokes to a cell. Smith is to be charged with suspected murder—and I don't think we'll have trouble digging up evidence to that effect—and this other trouble-maker—"

"Brooke is the name—Stony Brooke. And I'm going to see to it you don't forget the name, Nirvan—"

"Brooke," Nirvan snapped angrily, "is to be charged with being an accessory. When that's taken care of, Yarrow, you'd better go out and find the body Smith *claims* he found—"

"Jeepers! What a raw deal!" Johnny Jump-Up gasped.

"You, Johnny, keep your mouth shut, or it will be the worse for you one of these days—" Nirvan began.

"And I'll be found with a slash ripped across my forehead, eh?" Johnny said defiantly.

"By God," Nirvan rasped, "I'll—" He could scarcely continue for a moment, so great was his anger, then, "You hinting that I know something about those slash murders, Johnny?"

"If you don't, who does?" Johnny said bravely. "You claim to run this town. Who should know better than you. Anybody you don't get on with dies sudden, and the body is always found with that slash brand across the forehead. Me, I've been doing plenty of thinking, Matt, and it's always folks who buck you that get that mark."

Neutral customers in the saloon looked curiously at Nirvan. This was something that hadn't occurred to them before. Nirvan realized suddenly that too much talk was being made. He laughed shortly. "Johnny, you've sure got a powerful imagination, but you're all wrong, of course. You'd better think things over for a spell, and then change your mind." Neither Johnny, nor Tucson and his pard, missed the hidden threat in Nirvan's words.

Nirvan swung back to the sheriff. "What in hell you waiting for, Beef? I told you to get these two hombres to a cell. Get started, you hear me?"

Yarrow and Volpone advanced on Tucson and Stony, demanding their guns. Both men backed away, resolving to draw and shoot it out, rather than surrender their weapons. "Gawddammit!" Yarrow bellowed, "Have I got to ask you again to hand over those guns? I'll sure blast you to hell if you don't—"

"Quit the palaver, Beef!" Nirvan's tones were savage. "Those two are resisting a legally sworn officer. You know your duty—"

There came another interruption when a drawling voice cut in:

"Kind of looks like I just woke up in time. Dang you, Tucson and Stony, the minute I let you out of my sight, you get into trouble. And you other gents, with the guns in your hands, please put 'em away. They might go off by accident and then there'd be merry hell to pay."

Tucson's heart leaped. The room had swung about to learn the direction from which this fresh voice came. Lullaby Joslin stood just within the swinging doors. He yawned widely as he faced them, but the six-shooter in his right fist didn't waver a particle. Tucson and Stony grinned with relief. Back of them came Johnny's voice, breathless with emotion: "Good Lord, Tucson Smith, how many more have you got in your gang?"

"Enough," Tucson laughed. "Mister Nirvan might yet get a surprise if he knew how strong we are."

Again the tables had been turned and once more Tucson held the upper hand. Matt Nirvan, features contorted with rage, looked about to throw caution to the wind and go for his gun. As though reading the man's mind, Lullaby spoke:

"Don't try it, mister," he drawled sleepily, "I might get careless with this heat and fog it promiscuous."

Nirvan nodded shortly. He wasn't frightened,

but he knew when the odds were too great to be bucked. Slowly he returned his gun to its holster. "Maybe we'd all better cool down and talk things over," he suggested.

"Now you're talking sense," Tucson stated. He put out one hand and jerked the leather heel-lift from Yarrow's hand, then, to the bartender, "Johnny, would you mind coming around from your bar and trying this chunk of leather to Venner's boot. In that way, we'll get a real neutral opinion."

"With pleasure." Johnny rounded the bar and got the leather. Venner started to back away, his face pale, protesting his innocence.

"Damn you, Venner, hold still," Nirvan snapped. "We'll get to the bottom of this. Hold up your foot, blast you!"

Venner looked on the point of collapse. His eyes rolled appealingly toward Yarrow and Nirvan. Some sort of message passed between the men and Venner lifted his foot. Johnny stopped before him, and a moment later announced that the leather lift fitted Venner's boot heel "to a T, gents! And don't take my word for it. See for yourselves." Several men drew near, took one look and agreed with Johnny.

Tucson spoke sternly to Yarrow: "There's your proof, sheriff. And there's three of us here to prove we saw Venner and one other making a getaway after the killing. Could be that Wonch is the other man. Now if you'll take my advice you'll go out and get that body—"

"Yaah!" Yarrow spat angrily. "Who are you to be giving me orders? Hell, Venner might have lost that heel-lift at any time. Finding that near the body is no sign Venner had just dropped it. He might have lost it a week ago—"

"That's right," Venner interrupted in a trembling voice. "It's over a week, I'd say. I was riding over near the creek and—"

"You see, Smith," Yarrow started. "You just jumped to conclusions and—"

"Cut it, Beef," Nirvan snapped. "Don't make a bigger fool of yourself than you have already. Throw Venner in a cell until this matter's cleared up. Wonch too, until he can be questioned about his whereabouts today. Then you get out there *pronto*, and bring back that body."

The sheriff commenced a protest but a look from Nirvan shut him up. A moment later, Yarrow and Volpone were hustling Wonch and Venner toward cells, and the roomful of men breathed a collective sigh of relief. Matt Nirvan turned to Tucson, holding out his hand. "I want to apologize, Smith. I reckon I took too much stock in Beef Yarrow's story." He forced a smile. "I'm sorry now I acted as I did, but when I saw a stranger here holding a gun on our law officers, I just had to act and get matters cleared up. I really regret it."

"I'll bet you do," Lullaby spoke sleepily, "especially the way it ended."

Nirvan's skin took on a tinge of color, but he held his temper, hand still outstretched. Tucson was suddenly occupied with rolling a Bull Durham cigarette and failed to see the hand which Nirvan finally lowered. Nirvan said awkwardly, "I feel I should buy a drink for you boys. What'll you have. Johnny—!"

"Forget it, Nirvan. A drink isn't necessary. You spoke out of turn, but now you've seen your mistake. I reckon that finishes the matter." He lighted his cigarette and grinned cheerfully. "So with that settled, we can all start all even-steven again."

"Pretty decent of you to take it that way," Nirvan said. "Do you boys intend to be in Manzanita long?"

Tucson looked steadily at Nirvan a moment. "Yes, I think we will be. We hadn't figured to stay, but so long as Yarrow suspects me of doing that killing, I'd like to stay long enough to see myself cleared, and see justice done where the killer is concerned. If Venner and Wonch aren't guilty, I want to know who is."

"Fine," Nirvan nodded with a heartiness he was far from feeling. "Perhaps I can throw something in your way. I have considerable interests around here, and if you want a job—"

"Thanks, no," Tucson replied. "We're not

on the working list right now. Taking a sort of vacation as you might put it."

"You probably won't stay long then," Nirvan commented. "There's not much doing around Manzanita to interest three young fellows. You know, to tell the truth, I'm rather glad you put the bee on Venner and Wonch. I was just on the point of having Yarrow order them to leave town. They're a couple of no-goods—"

Tucson chuckled. "I seem to remember you called them 'two prominent citizens' a spell back, Nirvan. Changed your mind?"

"Well—er—that is—" Nirvan floundered, grinning sheepishly. "You see, Smith, that was just civic pride speaking. You came here as a stranger and started hurling accusations about two townspeople. Naturally, I felt a sort of loyalty to them. Of course, I should have known better. But I didn't stop to think, in the excitement and all—" He paused to mop his forehead with a black handkerchief. The man was plainly flustered. "Well," he changed the subject, "if you're going to be in town for a spell, drop around to the Purgatoire. That's my place. The games are honest, the girls pretty and the liquor prime. I'll be glad to have you pay us a visit."

"Sure," Tucson nodded. "We don't figure to overlook anything."

Nirvan looked sharply at Tucson, then at Lullaby and Stony. The men had assumed easy, careless postures. Lullaby appeared to be half asleep. Nirvan said, "Well, I've got to be getting along. I'll be seeing you around town. And I want to say again, I'm sorry this business happened as it did."

Lullaby's mouth opened in a jaw-breaking yawn. "I'll bet you are," he mumbled sleepily.

With no more words, Nirvan turned and departed from the Brown Bottle. He was scarcely out of sight when the other customers followed, drifting out singly and by twos. Within five minutes, only Tucson and his pardners, and Johnny Jump-up remained. No one spoke for a moment, then Johnny said, "Whew!" There was considerable relief in the tone, as the little man mopped perspiration from his face.

"What's the matter?" Tucson asked.

Johnny didn't answer directly. He said, "You three reckless fools got your broncs handy?"

"They're up the street a spell," Tucson replied.

"Well, you'd better run—not walk—and get 'em *muy pronto*! And climb in the saddles and get the hell out of Manzanita."

"How come?" from Stony.

"Right now," Johnny explained, "I wouldn't give a plugged nickel for your lives—all three of 'em. You've made an enemy of Matt Nirvan. Smart hombres don't do that. If they don't like him, they get out. Nirvan won't forget. Not since he's been here has anybody handled him the way you three did, and that was damnably hard for him to swallow. You'd better slope, gents."

Tucson laughed softly. "I remember you spoke back to him, too, Johnny."

"I haven't forgotten it," Johnny replied gloomily. "I like to forgot myself, I guess. But I got capital tied up in a business here. I don't intend to run off and leave the Brown Bottle. Nirvan has tried to buy me out two-three times, but after twenty years in the same location, I just can't bear to pass the business on to him. But maybe I'd better sell out for what I can get. There ain't no business worth a man's life—"

"Looked to me like your trade is spoiled anyway," Tucson pointed out, "the way your customers slunk out the instant Nirvan left."

"I didn't miss that." Johnny looked worried. "Speaking back to Nirvan the way I did, makes me a marked man, and fellers won't be anxious to be associated with me—"

"Nor with us three. I noticed they didn't act so afraid of Yarrow and his deputy, but Nirvan was a different proposition. I'm afraid we've spoiled your trade for you, Johnny."

"Maybe it was worth it," Johnny said dubiously.

Stony put in. "That being the case, Tucson, I figure we should stick around long enough to see that Johnny gets his trade back."

"Oh, Lord," Lullaby groaned, "you hombres are fixing to get into a mess again. There goes my peaceful nocturnal rest. But I suppose I'll have to stick around and pull you out of any tights you get into."

Tucson said grimly, "Maybe all our peace is about to be disturbed. Johnny, give us the layout around here. When we have some information we'll know better how to move. When we know how to move—well, maybe we can keep Nirvan on the jump too."

IV

"There's not much I can tell you," Johnny began slowly, "that's safe to tell. Every word I speak is likely to bring me that much nearer to a severe case of lead poisoning."

"Whatever you say won't go any further," Tucson promised. "Just who is Matt Nirvan, anyway?"

Johnny considered. "Actually, I've got a hunch he's a madman—the vicious sort. As I look back over the three years he's been in Manzanita I must admit I don't know much more about him than I did at first, when he arrived here. He looked exactly the same as he did today. He had a few hundred dollars, with which he bought the old Eagle Saloon and Gambling Parlor. With the aid of one barkeep and a faro dealer, he operated the place until he could get some money ahead. The old Eagle had been run honestly. After Nirvan took over it was mighty unusual for any hombre to win any money there. Gunfights became frequent, with Nirvan always holding the winning guns—"

"Fast with his hardware, eh?" Tucson said.

Johnny nodded. "I've never seen anyone faster, and I've seen many of the oldtime gunfighters in action. But Nirvan's speed and accuracy is uncanny."

"Uncanned," Lullaby corrected lazily. "Well, Johnny, we three make a specialty of canning hard hombres, so we're not scared so far."

Johnny said moodily, "Then you're a lot different from most people hereabouts. Anyway, after Nirvan made a paying proposition out of the old Eagle, he remodeled it, imported some painted hussies and guntoters, and renamed it the Purgatoire."

"That's a hell of a name," Stony commented.

"It's a money-coining hell," Johnny said. "As Nirvan grew richer, he broadened his activities. He bought one of the general stores here, giving his note, but beyond his down-payment, no more money ever changed hands. Tod Holden, the man who held Nirvan's note, was shot to death. The day after Holden was killed, Nirvan produced a paid-in-full receipt, which Holden's widow called a forgery, but she couldn't prove it, of course. By that time Nirvan had too strong a hold on this town. Holden was the first man to be found with that red slash cut across his forehead. I've a hunch that Nirvan did it during some sort of insane rage, then decided it was a good trademark to terrorize folks with."

"You're sure Nirvan killed Holden?" Tucson asked.

Johnny shook his head. "No proof. I just suspicion it. Next two owners of saloons died sudden, when they refused to sell out to Nirvan.

They'd both been slashed across the forehead. After their funerals, Nirvan produced bills-of-sale for their places, too."

Stony asked, "Johnny, didn't you say Nirvan had been trying to buy your place?"

Johnny Jump-Up nodded. "I'm not feeling so good about that, neither. I keep a sawed-off scatter-gun under the bar and I never move far away from it. There was a mine payroll stage routed through here one time. The messenger was killed—forehead slashed—and the money taken. Next, Nirvan tried to buy Charley Young's Lazy-Y outfit, but Charley refused to sell. So Charley got the usual dose and again Nirvan produced a bill-of-sale for the place. Since then, honest people speak of the Lazy-Y as the Snake's Tongue outfit. But never within Nirvan's hearing."

"Looks like Nirvan is building himself his own little empire hereabouts," Tucson said.

"God, that's the truth!" Johnny agreed. "The money is rolling in and he grows stronger all the time. He runs Manzanita all right. Calls it his own town—boasts of the fact that he runs things to suit himself. Claims that he's running out the rough characters, whereas more and more of them seem to be brought in. Both Yarrow and Volpone are under his thumb. He rigged the election and put them into office, two years back."

"It's a wonder to me," Tucson remarked, "that

the decent men of the town don't rise against him."

"A few did, but before they could get an organization going, they died sudden. What I'm trying to impress on you is this—while there's no actual proof against Nirvan, every time some hombre crosses him, said hombre dies. And that red slash brand is always found on his forehead. Folks are sure scary about that."

"Sweet layout," Tucson scowled. "One wolf ravaging the whole Manzanita country, and no one daring to down the beast. I'm wondering about the identity of the dead man we found today."

Johnny looked concerned. "I've been worried about that too."

"Worried?" Stony asked.

Johnny explained, "For the past year Nirvan has been trying to buy Sam Dixon's Wagon-Wheel Ranch. Sam and his daughter—Sam's wife is dead—have a nice spread, land and buildings, the nicest around here. Their holdings are watered by Cottonwood Creek, and it's a regular cowman's paradise. I know Sam has refused to sell on several occasions. That's Nirvan's game—he makes a heap of talk about buying a place, then after the owner is dead, Nirvan shows up with the paper that says he had really put the deal across. And nobody can prove otherwise."

"The man must be insane," Tucson said,

frowning. He described to Johnny the appearance of the dead man they'd found that day.

Johnny's face fell. "God, I hope not, but I admit that description fits Sam Dixon to a T. It'll sure be tough on Louise, if—"

"Who's Louise?" Stony asked.

"Sam's daughter. If it is Sam who was killed and Nirvan doesn't show up with a bill-of-sale for the Wagon-Wheel, I sure feel skeery for Louise."

"Meaning Nirvan wouldn't hesitate to finish off the girl too?" Lullaby asked. "Hell, that's hard to believe."

"You don't know Nirvan," Johnny said grimly.

"So," Tucson growled, "maybe we'd best stick around and learn this madman."

"Oh, no," Lullaby protested. "I'm afraid we might get slashed across the forehead."

"I know just how afraid you are," Stony said. "But with the sort of head you got, you'd never know it anyway. Where there's no sense, there's no feeling."

Tucson broke in, "Johnny, we got involved in this business through no wish of our own, but now we're in it, I think we'd best see it through. We came here peaceful and got jumped on. Trouble here is that everybody acts afraid to buck Nirvan. If folks would just stick together and defy him openly, I've a hunch he can be handled."

"You actually going to stay and war openly on Nirvan?" Johnny asked nervously.

"I reckon so. You with us, Johnny?"

Johnny shrank back, then stiffened. "I'm scared to death," he confessed, "but I'm with you, fellers."

"That's the spirit, Johnny," Stony exclaimed, "and maybe you don't need to get too scared. You haven't seen Tucson in action—"

"Nor Stony and Lullaby," Tucson interrupted, reddening slightly. "We've had luck in a few past brawls. Maybe the luck will continue. C'mon, you two, let's go find some chow. My belly's beginning to think somebody's cut my throat." He started toward the doorway, followed by Lullaby and Stony, Johnny calling after them:

"Don't take any chances, fellows. Play it safe. Remember, if you get careless, there's many a slip between the cup and the lip."

"And between the gun and the hip," Stony pointed out, "and I aim to keep my holster slippery."

They reached the street, Lullaby muttering dolefully, "More trouble on the trail. You two will yet be the death of me."

V

Meanwhile, Matt Nirvan sat glowering in his private office at the rear of the Purgatoire honkytonk. Beyond the room there was a scattering of men at the bar, none of the games were in operation at this time of day and all of the girls were absent. From his position behind his flat-topped desk, Nirvan sat like a lean black spider considering his henchmen ranged before him and awaiting his orders.

There were seven men facing him: Black Payette, Shive Otis, a swarthy individual known only as Santone, Bronc Rabideau, Riker Wetzel, Snake Corelli and Gage Kraft. Nirvan's gunmen were hard-bitten men with sinewy jaws, bronzed features and thin-slitted eyes. Fast-drawing, quick-shooting men, all, who willingly accepted Nirvan's money to carry out black deeds they never questioned. All wore six-shooters, slouch brim sombreros and other clothing typical of the cow country.

Snake Corelli alone, in the matter of dress, stood out from his companions. A beaded chinstrap was attached to his sombrero. His spurs were inlaid with beaten silver. He wore a vivid blue silk shirt and the handkerchief knotted at his throat was of a brilliant purple. Corelli considered himself a dandy and spent considerable time twisting the waxed ends of the small black mustache on his upper lip.

While not the fastest gun in the outfit, Corelli was considered the dirtiest fighter. Where one or two of the others possessed compunctions regarding shooting an opponent in the back, Corelli considered them squeamish for holding such ideas. Even his own companions, including Matt Nirvan, trusted him only so far.

Nirvan shoved a bottle and glasses across the desk. “Help yourselves,” he growled. The men poured drinks, consumed them, wiped their lips, and considered the situation.

“I don’t see, Matt,” Riker Wetzel said placatingly, “why you got to take this business so much to heart. No need for you to get so riled up about three strange cow-waddies. We can handle ’em.”

“You didn’t have their guns covering you, like I did,” Nirvan snapped. “It’s a long, long time since anybody dropped a gun on *me* that way. And I didn’t like it. I still don’t.”

Santone said philosophically, “No use crying over spilt liquor, boss. Look here, that cowpoke came up behind you, unawares. And as you tell it, this Brooke hombre got the drop on Beef and Trent Volpone the same way. Any kid could do that much. Those bastards were just lucky.”

“Admitted,” Nirvan said irritably, “but there

was no luck in the way that Tucson Smith handled both Wonch and Venner at the same time. That pair isn't bad with their guns, but, as I heard it, Smith just plain outguessed them. Everybody knows they were working for me, so now I won't dast produce a bill-of-sale for Dixon's Wagon-Wheel. Instead I got to keep Venner and Wonch in jail until we can get things fixed with that trio of cowhands. Funny thing is, they don't look hard. Then, later, we'll have to take care of Dixon's daughter, somehow. Right now we'll have to go slow."

Snake Corelli gave his mustache a twirl. "Why don't you leave that girl to me, Matt? I can take care of females any time."

"Those three got to be taken care of first," Nirvan stated angrily,

Riker Wetzel spoke again. Wetzel was accepted as Nirvan's right hand man. "So all right, Matt. We're waiting for your orders regarding Smith and his two pards."

"Oh, hell," Black Payette growled, "I don't know why four or five of us can't just plug those three hombres. What we wasting all this talk about?"

Nirvan shook his head. "Not four or five, Blackie. Three will be enough. It's got to look like an even fight. We don't dast make things look too raw. There's still a few hombres left in this town that are ready to buck me. Three can pick a fight with Smith and his pards and settle the business, and nobody'll be able to scream 'Murder!' "

"Matt's correct," Gage Kraft nodded. "Count me as one of the three, Matt, to down those cow-nurses."

"And me," Shive Otis put in. "I could use some extra money."

"Not you, Shive," Nirvan shook his head. "You're more valuable for your knife work. I want someone faster with a gun. Lemme see. Gage, you can go."

"I'd sort of like to see how fast this Tucson hombre is," Bronc Rabideau said.

"Me, too," from Snake Corelli.

Nirvan nodded. "Good. That's three of you. Now here's my plan—"

At that moment there was a knock at the door and at Nirvan's "Come in!" a man with a hangdog appearance entered. "What is it, Pete?" Nirvan snapped. Pete was tall, slovenly, in shabby togs.

"Them three cowhands has left the Brown Bottle," Pete stated. "First they took their broncs to the livery for oats and a rubdown. Next they went to the Paris Restaurant for food. They're in the Paris joint now."

"Good, Pete." Nirvan tossed a silver dollar to the man who quickly left, closing the door behind him. Nirvan swung back to his henchmen. "Corelli, Rabideau and Kraft will be enough to handle those three. Here's the set-up. Drift down near the Paris Restaurant and wait for them to leave. Pick an argument with them somehow. I'll leave that to you. Corelli, you know plenty of fighting words. You start it. Just don't give 'em a chance to draw on you, but make things look right, understand?"

"We've got to see what they look like first," Gage Kraft pointed out. "Remember, Matt, we've never laid eyes on 'em."

"Forget that. You won't have any trouble locating them." He quickly described Tucson and his pardners. The three nodded and started to leave, but Nirvan called them back. "Better each have a drink first, boys. Not that you need Dutch courage, but sometimes it helps."

Drinks were poured. Nirvan lifted his glass. "Here's to a fast departure for three nosy cowpokes who didn't know enough to leave town when they had a chance. Drink hearty!"

VI

The plan was somewhat altered, however, when Snake Corelli felt he must make certain of his proposed victims' identity. He couldn't resist the temptation to get a good look at them before the time came for the arranged fight. Leaving Gage Kraft and Bronc Rabideau behind, he swaggered down the main street until he had reached the Paris Restaurant, a small place with tables and a counter at one side. At the present moment the windows were somewhat steamed, and Corelli couldn't get the view he wished for.

Tucson and his companions were seated at a corner table in the restaurant. Two other customers dawdled over coffee at the counter. The Mesquiteers were about through and were forking up chunks of cherry pie, when Snake Corelli pushed through the entrance and paused at a small tobacco case near the front to purchase a sack of Bull Durham. While awaiting his change from the proprietor, he turned to get a good look at Tucson and his friends.

Tucson wasn't missing that long stare. He sat facing Corelli; Lullaby and Stony were seated at the opposite side of the table, their backs to the front of the restaurant. Tucson met Corelli's glance for a brief moment, then reached for his cup. He lifted it to his lips, eyes taking in every detail of Corelli's appearance, while the gunman was twisting his neck for a better view of Stony and Lullaby.

Receiving his change, Corelli took a long last glance at the three and, spurs clanking across the floor, left the restaurant, the door slamming behind him.

Tucson laughed softly, putting down his coffee cup. "Things are commencing to tighten a mite, looks like."

Lullaby and Stony looked up from their pie plates. "In what way?" Stony asked.

"I've a hunch Nirvan has put some hired gun-slingers on our trail," Tucson replied. "They'll probably pick a fight with us when we leave here, with full intentions of carrying it through to a finish. Maybe we're sort of in for it."

"Hell!" Stony said casually. "I never did expect to live forever."

Lullaby yawned sleepily. "Say, did you two notice what a swell piece of cherry pie that was? Let's have another piece."

Stony chuckled. "Figuring to die on a full stomach, Lullaby?"

Lullaby drawled, "Don't always be pestering me with such minor details, lunkhead. It's Nirvan that's due to get a bellyful if he don't quit bothering me. And I don't intend to have my meal interrupted with any such morbid thoughts. . . . Hey, prop! How's about some more java and another piece of pie?" The proprietor came hustling with the order.

The sun was swinging toward the serrated peaks of the Labajada Mountains, when the three men emerged from the eating house. Tucson glanced along the street. The distance of half a city block away, he saw Corelli and two other tough-looking characters loitering in front of a harness shop.

Tucson rolled a cigarette while he spoke low-voiced to Stony and Lullaby. "They're waiting for us," he said, "three of 'em, including that gaudy dressed hombre that came in for tobacco while we were waiting. They probably figure to bump into us, throw some rough language our way, as we pass by. Then when we object, they'll draw and plug us. But I don't feel like cooperating. Follow my lead and let's see what happens."

He swung off along the street, with Stony and Lullaby on each side of him. Now that the worst heat of the day had passed, a few people were emerging from houses and were passing along on either side of the street. Tucson and his companions appeared in no hurry as they strolled; apparently they hadn't a care in the world, their arms swinging easily at their sides.

Corelli and the other two watched Tucson and his friends approach, their eyes narrowing in anticipation. "Here they come," Corelli snapped. He moved quickly away from the front of the harness shop and into the passageway between the shop and an adjoining hay and feed store. Rabideau and Gage Kraft were close on his heels. The three waited, out of view of the street, between the two buildings, thumbs hooked in cartridge belts.

"They'll be here now, any minute," Corelli whispered hoarsely. "You fellers be ready. I'll wait until Smith and his pards are passing then I'll call him a—!" He voiced an unprintable epithet. "When they stop to object, we'll let 'em have it. All clear?"

The other two nodded, tensing a little, hands moving closer to gunbutts.

The footsteps of Tucson and his companions sounded nearer. Corelli was already opening his mouth to yell at Tucson, when the words ended in a startled squawk. Instead of moving past the passageway, as Corelli expected, Tucson rounded the corner of the building and entered the passageway, Stony and Lullaby close at his shoulders. The guns of all three were already out and leveled.

"Surprise!" Tucson announced. "We're beating you to the punch, hombres! Just lift those paws up from your holsters if you know what's good for you."

The three gunmen stared, eyes wide, jaws

sagging, but lost to time in lifting their arms shoulder-high.

"Wha—wha—what's the idea of this?" Gage Kraft stammered. "We ain't had any trouble with you."

Corelli swore. "You're just making things tough for yourselves," he threatened. "When Matt Nirvan hears—"

"We've already had one run-in with Nirvan and a couple of his coyotes," Tucson snapped, "so it wasn't hard to put two and two together and get three—three would-be badmen waiting to do some backshooting. Three skunks that sure as hell are due to be taught a lesson—"

The words weren't finished, as Corelli, taking a desperate chance, flashed his right hand toward his holster. Before he could draw something was jammed hard against his middle. A painful grunt was expelled from his open mouth as Tucson's gun barrel bored in below the breastbone.

"I should shoot, but I won't this time," Tucson stated harshly. "But we already had the drop on you and we aren't lowdown enough to take advantage of that fact. But don't make that mistake a second time, mister, or sure as hell you'll get drilled."

Corelli's arms were high again, his eyes bulging with fright. "Th—th—this is all a mistake," he stuttered.

"It sure was," Tucson agreed. He spoke to his

two companions: "Keep these buzzards covered," then he returned to Corelli, "What's your name?"

"Corelli?"

"Corelli, *sir!*" Stony corrected. "You say *sir* when the other man's got the advantage, dumbhead."

Corelli gulped. "Corelli, sir."

"That's better," Tucson smiled. "Who's your friends?"

"Bronc Rabideau and Gage Kraft—sir."

"Fine," Tucson nodded. "We'll remember those names. Now listen close, Corelli. You go back to Matt Nirvan and tell him war is declared. He's been running Manzanita in pretty highhanded fashion. Could be it's none of our business, but he insisted in nosing into our affairs, so we aim to show you coyotes exactly what 'highhanded' means. Would-be tough hombres like you three, we eat for breakfast, after first tendering 'em up a mite—"

"You—!" Corelli could contain his temper no longer, as he voiced a vile epithet.

Tucson's features tightened. Shoving his six-shooter back in the holster he reached up and fastened his fingers in the beaded chinstrap of Corelli's sombrero. Then his grip slowly tightened.

"You're yellow, Corelli," Tucson stated, level-voiced. "You knew I wouldn't pull trigger on you, much as I wanted to. But I sure aim to teach you a lesson."

He commenced to turn his clenched fist, gripping the chinstrap. As his grasp tightened, turning, the chinstrap likewise tightened. Corelli tried to cry out, but the taut chinstrap was cutting off his wind. He struggled, gasping for breath, but Tucson held him in a grip of iron. Corelli's face began to purple, his knees sagged. Only Tucson's grip held him erect now.

Then Tucson lifted his gun from its holster, using his other hand. "I understand," Tucson said grimly, "that it's the custom of Nirvan's men to tear a slash across the foreheads of their victims. Well, two can play at that game—"

He shifted the grip on his gun and swiftly drew the sight of the weapon in a diagonal line across Corelli's forehead. With force behind it, the gunsight tore an ugly, jagged gash in the skin.

"Check!" Tucson snapped, then drew a second diagonal slash across the first, making a crude X, "—and double-check!" he concluded. Rabideau and Kraft watched the performance with wide eyes, but said nothing.

Tucson released his hold on Corelli's chinstrap and allowed the man to fall, staggering, against the wall of the nearby building. Corelli sank down, lungs struggling for breath, the crimson X on his forehead welling with blood.

"That's all," Tucson said tonelessly. "I've got

you marked, Corelli. Next time you cut my trail, you'd better be ready to smoke your gun, because I'll do your next branding with one of Mister Sam Colt's lead slugs." He swung back to Lullaby and Stony. "Take their guns," he said shortly, "but let Corelli keep his. In case he figures to square this account I don't want to have him wasting time buying new equipment."

Lullaby and Stony quickly disarmed Kraft and Rabideau, while the two glared helplessly at them. Tucson laughed softly, but his tone carried nothing of humor. "This is just a beginning, hombres. Go on back to Nirvan and tell him he isn't the only one can play this gun-branding game."

Kraft and Rabideau didn't reply. Corelli held himself erect with an effort. "Damn you, Smith," he said venomously, "someday I'll have your heart for this." With the back of one trembling hand he wiped blood from his forehead.

"Take my advice and you won't even try," Tucson said contemptuously. "Come on Stony—Lullaby. We'll let lesson number one sink in, before we start our next teaching."

The three turned back to the street and headed toward the Brown Bottle. The action, hidden as it was between buildings, had gone unnoticed by passers-by on the walks.

The instant the Mesquiteers had left, Corelli, cursing insanely, drew his gun and leaped toward the street. Before he could reach the walk, Kraft and Rabideau seized his arms and held him back.

"Don't be a damned fool, Snake," Rabideau panted, as Corelli strove to break loose. "You can't see for the blood in your eyes now. You'd be an easy mark for that blasted red-headed cowpoke."

"And remember," Kraft pointed out, "we'd be no help to you, Snake. We ain't got our guns. By God, someday I'll shoot that Smith so full of holes—all three of them bastards—"

Rabideau was the coolest of the three. "We'd best get back to the Purgatoire as soon as possible and get that cut on Snake's head fixed up."

"Matt ain't going to like it," Kraft said nervously.

"I don't like it, either," Rabideau snapped, "but I've got to admit we underestimated those three. We'll just have to make another plan. What none of us have realized is that those cowpokes are hard as nails. It was their easy ways that fooled us. I don't aim to be fooled a second time."

VII

Except for Tucson and his companions, the Brown Bottle was entirely devoid of customers when they arrived. Johnny Jump-Up slouched dejectedly at one end of his bar. The sun was gone now, and oil lamps, suspended on wall brackets, illuminated the barroom. Johnny forced a smile when they entered. "Customers at last—I hope."

"Your hope is due to be fulfilled," Lullaby said lazily. "Set 'em out, barkeep. What's wrong? No business?"

"Business is all plumb shot to the bad place," Johnny admitted morosely.

"I reckon that's our fault," Tucson said. "Want we should leave, Johnny?"

"Hell, no," Johnny said loyally. "And it's not all your fault. I should've known better than to have shot off my mouth."

"Tell you what you do," Tucson proposed, "you go to Nirvan and apologize. The guns we took off Rabideau and Kraft you can give back and that will maybe put him in a good humor—"

"Guns? What guns you talking about?"

"Rabideau's hawg-laig," Stony said, placing the weapon on the bar.

"And Kraft's," Lullaby replied, following suit.

"Hey, hey," Johnny's features took on a look of

excitement. “What’s been going on? You had a brush with those two?”

Tucson told what had happened, Johnny’s eyes widening meanwhile, his jaw dropping in amazement. “Moses on the Mountain!” he exclaimed when Tucson had concluded. He seemed unable to speak further but immediately busied himself setting out drinks. “This is one case when not only the first drink is free. Judas Priest on a Mule! Now you have got something started. And you handled those three that easy? Damn, that’s hard to believe.” He was beaming widely. “T’hell with business, if you boys can do something like that—”

“Say, Tucson,” Stony broke in, “now I know why you left the restaurant right after we ordered and went to the general store for a file. While you were away, you sharpened up your gunsight!”

“Correct,” Tucson nodded. “It’s a lending file in case you two want to borrow it. The way I see it, we’ve got to show ourselves just as ruthless as the Nirvan gang. It’s the only sort of force they’ll be able to understand.”

“What’s this about a file?” Johnny asked curiously.

Lullaby explained in languid tones, “You know that slash that’s always left on the foreheads of Nirvan’s victims. Well, Tucson adds an extra slash to cancel out the Nirvan mark—a sort of ‘X marks the spot’ idea.”

"You—you mean," Johnny stammered, "you branded Corelli with your gunsight?" Tucson nodded. Johnny exclaimed, "Oh, my God! What next?"

Tucson scratched his head. "That's what I'm wondering too."

Lullaby said, "Let's go back to the Paris and get some more pie. I'm hungry."

"Eat and sleep. That's all you think of," Stony jeered.

"Can you think of anything better to do?" Lullaby asked mildly.

Tucson said, "Lullaby's right. We'd best get out and move around a mite. Maybe Johnny's trade will pick up. C'mon, pards. See you later, Johnny."

"Hey," Johnny said, pointing to the weapons Stony and Lullaby had left on his bar, "what'll I do with these guns?"

"Stick 'em in your back-bar drawer," Tucson suggested. "If Rabideau and Kraft want 'em, let 'em have their smoke-wagons." He nodded again and the three men departed.

After stopping at the restaurant for more pie and coffee, the trio just wandered around town, senses alert for any sign of hostility, but none showed. Mostly by this time the town was dark. Yellow rectangles of light showed from windows here and there. Most of the saloons seemed to be doing good business. A few pedestrians passed, or a cowhand on a horse loped down the center of the road. Lullaby finally complained that he was tired of walking and that he needed a beer, so the trio returned to the Brown Bottle Saloon. This time when they entered, three men stood at the bar and Johnny looked more cheerful.

Tucson and his friends gave their orders. Bottles of beer were set out. The other customers stole curious side glances at the Mesquiteers. One of them finally said to Johnny in a louder voice than necessary, "Heard there was a little fracas in town just before sundown, Johnny. Did you hear any details?"

Uncertain how to answer, Johnny looked at Tucson. Tucson laughed shortly. "My friends and I had a little run-in with three of Nirvan's plug-uglies. It didn't amount to much."

"And you're still here?" another man asked. He looked aghast.

"Haven't seen any reason for moving on, yet," Lullaby said lazily.

Tucson asked, "Where'd you hear about it, mister?"

The man shrugged. "I'm not sure. There's just a rumor floating about. I guess it couldn't have been serious."

"It wasn't," Tucson said agreeably. "Ask Snake Corelli about it when you see him—or maybe you won't see him until he heals."

"Heals?"

"He had a nasty accident," Stony supplied. "Nothing much—just got an X-shaped cut on his forehead."

The three customers looked quickly at each other, finished their drinks and left hurriedly. Tucson said regretfully, "There goes more of Johnny's business."

"Damn it, it's worth it," Johnny said spiritedly. "Leastwise folks will begin to learn that somebody's bucking Nirvan at last." He frowned. "I mean that. You fellows have given Nirvan something to think about. Kraft, Corelli and Rabideau are considered bad men to tangle with. I'm betting you've thrown a shock into Nirvan and he'll do a lot of thinking before he makes his next move."

At that moment the hangdog character named Pete who'd been in Nirvan's office entered the barroom. He was rather smut-faced and slouching in appearance. Johnny said, "Howdy, Pete. Any news?"

"Bad news," Pete replied. He glanced curiously at Tucson and his friends.

Johnny said, "Pete was in here this afternoon after you left to eat. I asked him to let me know when Beef Yarrow and Trent Volpone returned with the body of that murdered man you found this morning. Pete, what's the answer?"

"Yarrow and Volpone got back," Pete said. "They brought in Sam Dixon's body. Like so many others, there was that red slash on the forehead."

"Sam Dixon?" Johnny's face twisted with emotion. "That's hell. I thought a lot of Sam. I was sort of afraid it might be him, though."

"The owner of the Wagon-Wheel outfit, eh?" Stony asked.

"That's right," Johnny said dumbly. "It's sure bad news all right." He turned back to Pete, tossing a four-bit piece on the bar. "Have a drink, Pete?"

"I could stand one." Pete shuffled up to the bar. Johnny poured a tumbler full of whiskey which the man downed, without setting down the glass. Johnny thanked him for bringing the news. Pete said, "It's nothing." He picked the fifty-cent piece from the bar, but made no move to depart. Instead he rolled a cornhusk cigarette and lounged against one end of the bar, watching Tucson and his companions.

Johnny said, "Pete, did Yarrow send anybody out to the Wagon-Wheel with the news?"

Pete shoved his battered felt hat to one side and said no, adding, "I heard him say that maybe in a couple of days or so, if he could find time, he would ride to the Wagon-Wheel and tell the girl, hisself."

"That's just like Yarrow," Johnny said angrily. "Sam's daughter is likely worried about Sam's not returning home, right now. That fat slob of a badge-wearing son-of-a—" He broke off. "I guess I'd better close up and ride out and tell Louise myself, much as I hate it."

"I'll run the bar for you," Lullaby offered. "I've already had some bar experience—"

"He sure has, Johnny," Stony cut in, "but from this side of the bar. Cripes A'mighty! Johnny hasn't got any trade now. If he let you 'tend the place, he wouldn't have any stock, either, by the time he got back."

"Aw, go soak your head in a fish-barrel," Lullaby growled good-naturedly.

Tucson said thoughtfully, glancing meaningly at his pardners, "I don't think it would be a good idea for Johnny to make that ride tonight." Stony and Lullaby nodded understanding of the words. Tucson continued, "I'm not keen on the job of being the one to break bad news, but I think it might be a good idea to get acquainted with the Wagon-Wheel outfit. Excepting Johnny, we've made nothing but enemies since we struck this burg. I'd like to make a few friends for a change."

"That's just like you to suggest a ride like that tonight," Lullaby groaned. "And me figuring to catch up on my shut-eye too." Another groan. "Oh, well, I've heard of human sacrifices, so I'll just have to make up my mind to see what it's like. When do we start?"

"You don't," Tucson said. "You stay here with Johnny. Stony and I will make the ride to the Wagon-Wheel—"

"Look here, Tucson," Johnny interrupted. "I can take care of myself. It's not necessary that Lullaby stay here with me."

"I know it's not necessary," Tucson smiled, "but I'll feel better if you have some insurance here, in case Nirvan decides to play rough. And I want a man to stay here and keep an eye open."

"Have it your way," Johnny shrugged. "I've got an extra cot in my back room."

"Then Lullaby won't keep any eye open," Stony snickered.

"To hell with you, you flat-headed sheep-herder," Lullaby growled. "I'm not as dumb as you look—"

"Quit scrapping, you two," Tucson broke in. "It's settled then. Lullaby stays here. Stony and I ride to the Wagon-Wheel. Johnny, how much of a ride is it?"

"Not so far." Johnny gave directions, adding, "When you get there, ask for Ringbone Tilford. He's the foreman and one right old codger."

Tucson nodded. "Stony, let's drift over to the livery and get our broncs. The sooner we start, the sooner we get there."

At the same moment, Pete decided to leave. "I think I'll go find some place to sleep," he announced. "G'night." Shuffling feet carried him through the swinging doors.

Tucson glanced sharply after the man. "Who's that Pete hombre, Johnny?"

Johnny shrugged. "I don't know much about him. Pretty much of a bum, I reckon. He hangs around town and cadges drinks and runs errands for folks. I don't know where he sleeps. Any place he happens to sag down, I imagine."

"I wouldn't trust him too far," Tucson observed.

Lullaby drawled, "My sentiments exactly. You'll notice that while most folks have been steering clear of the Brown Bottle, since Johnny spoke up to Nirvan, it doesn't bother Pete any. So he must feel safe coming here. I figure he's in Nirvan's pay."

"Could be," Tucson agreed. Johnny looked worried. Tucson said, "C'mon, Stony. Let's get started." They said "*Adios*," and hurried in the direction of the livery stable.

Pete shuffled, stoop-shouldered, along the street until he'd entered the wide double-doored entrance of the Purgatoire. It was a big barn-like structure filled with sounds of revelry. Men lined the bar. Poker chips clattered, wheels whirred. A small orchestra at the rear made music to which short-skirted, rouged women danced in the arms of clumsy-footed men. There was the clinking of glasses and shrill feminine laughter. Tobacco smoke floated like a pall halfway to the ceiling, making dim the string of oil lamps suspended there.

Pete pushed through the crowd and after

knocking, passed into Nirvan's office, closing the door at his rear. Nirvan sat at his desk. Riker Wetzel and Snake Corelli occupied chairs nearby. A broad X of flesh-colored court-plaster decorated Corelli's forehead. Nirvan snapped, "What's kept you, Pete?"

The man cringed before Nirvan's scowl. "Sorry, Mister Nirvan, but I ain't learned nothing to report up to now. Smith and his two pals have been hanging 'round the Brown Bottle most of the time. They went to the Paris once, and then took a walk, then went back to Johnny's place—"

"Who'd they talk to when they went walking?"

"Nobody, Mister Nirvan. I stuck close on their heels but they looked like they was just looking the town over. So I followed 'em back to the bar. When Yarrow brought that body in, I went and told Johnny—"

"What in hell for?" Nirvan demanded.

Pete cringed a little lower. "He give me four-bits to let him know who Beef brought in. Johnny wanted to know who'd been killed."

"Working for both of us, eh?" Nirvan said angrily.

"Got to make my eats where I can, Mister Nirvan—"

"Oh, hell!" Nirvan spun a silver dollar on his desk. "What else did you learn?"

"Smith and Brooke are heading for the Wagon-

Wheel. They'd be saddling up about now—"

"That's a break for us!" Nirvan leaped to his feet, obsidian-like eyes shining. "Now we'll get two of those hombres for sure. Snake, you want another crack at Smith?"

"You're wasting time asking me," Corelli said sullenly. He jammed on his sombrero. "What's the orders?"

"Good man! I reckon Gage and Bronc feel like you do. This time it will be three guns against two. Riker, get out to the bar and bring back Gage and Bronc. I'll outline things for Snake while you're gone. Pete, you get out back and throw saddles on three fast horses."

"Right, Mister Nirvan," Pete nodded, hurrying out close behind Riker Wetzel.

Nirvan whirled back to Corelli. "Don't take any chances this time, Snake. You take Bronc and Gage and ride fast to Cottonwood Creek. You know that spot where the trail dips down to cross the stream—"

Corelli's eyes glowed. "I ought to. I was hid there that time I bumped off Holden—"

"You needn't bring that up," Nirvan said testily. "Anyway, you three men cross the stream and hide in the brush. You'll have to ride fast to get there before Smith and Brooke, but you can do it. Wait there until they show up. You'll have a clear shot just as they enter the stream to cross. Don't miss your chance this time. And Kraft and

Rabideau are anxious to try out their new guns."

Corelli grinned evilly. "This is going to be almost too easy. What I'll do to that Smith—say, what about that Joslin hombre? He's staying behind—"

"I'm not forgetting Joslin. I'm working out something else to take care of both him and Johnny Jump-Up—"

The office door swung open. Riker Wetzel, followed by Kraft and Rabideau entered. "I hear we're due to get another crack at Smith—" Kraft began.

"Snake will explain it. Now get going—fast! There's no time to lose." The three hurried from the office without further talk, almost colliding with Pete who had returned to report that the horses were saddled and ready.

Pete asked Nirvan. "You got anythin' more for me to do?"

"You head back and keep an eye on the Brown Bottle. After the place has closed, see if you can find out if Joslin stays there with Johnny. Then come back and let me know."

Out back of the Purgatoire, Rabideau, Kraft and Corelli found the saddled horses waiting in the shadows. The moon hadn't yet climbed above the horizon. As the three were getting into their rigs, Riker Wetzel came hurrying through the gloom. "I just gave a look down toward the livery," Wetzel whispered hoarsely. "Smith and Brooke have just started. Swing down this side street to the west, and then wide of town. Those two cowpokes won't be riding fast, 'cause they're strange to the trail. But you hombres make time and hit Cottonwood Creek before they do. And fill them so full of slugs when they show up, they won't even make good sieves."

"Leave it to us," Corelli spoke confidently. "They won't slip anything over on us this time, Riker."

Ten minutes later, Corelli and his two companions had left the lights of Manzanita far to the rear. Their ponies swung swiftly along, urged on by cruel spurs. Another fifteen minutes passed before Corelli called to his companions, then headed at a tangent toward the south. Before long the trio of gunmen had reached the wheel-rutted, hoof-chopped trail that ran to the Wagon-Wheel Ranch. Once more they straightened their course, urging their mounts along beneath the star-encrusted night.

It required little short of an hour for them to reach Cottonwood Creek. The horses slowed pace, dipped down the short slope to the water's edge, pushed across and emerged, with dripping stirrups, on the opposite side which was lined thickly with brush and cottonwood trees. Corelli led the way back under leafy boughs which rustled softly in the night breeze, and gave the word to dismount.

"Grab your Winchesters," Corelli said, low-voiced. "We'll save our Colts for close-up work, after we've first downed 'em."

The three men left their ponies and moved back to the brush at the edge of the creek, where grew a tangled thicket of mesquite, prickly-pear and long grass, affording a good hiding place for ambushers. Corelli and the other two settled down to wait.

After a time, Gage Kraft moved stiffly. "Dammit, I wish them two would hurry up."

"Getting nervous?" Rabideau laughed softly. "You've got no reason to be. We've got a leadpipe-cinch this time, Gage."

"No, I ain't nervous," Kraft commenced, "only—"

"Shhh!" Corelli hissed. "They're coming. I hear 'em."

The three crouched lower in the brush, tensely waiting. From beyond the slope on the opposite side of the smoothly flowing creek, came the sounds of thudding hoofs, the creaking of saddle leather and two voices raised in good-humored argument.

"That's Smith's voice," Corelli whispered, in a voice that trembled with hate and excitement. "Get your guns ready, and give 'em hell the instant they step their ponies into the creek. We can't miss 'em. They'll be sky-lighted when they top the rise."

VIII

Three muffled clicks sounded softly through the night as Corelli and his companions drew back the hammers on their Winchesters. The sound of approaching horses drew nearer. "Don't shoot too soon," Corelli cautioned in a hoarse whisper. "Wait until they've struck water. They'll be close enough then so we can't miss."

The three straightened to a half crouch in the brush, rifles at ready. They couldn't hear voices now, but the thudding of horses' hoofs drew nearer, the animals slowing down now as they approached the stream. Corelli strained his eyes against the opposite bank where the undulating earthline was silhouetted faintly against the starry night. Even while he watched, the heads of two horses appeared, bodies rising behind them. In the faint light from the stars, Corelli could distinguish the two figures on the horses' backs.

Corelli tensed. At his side he heard Kraft's quick, nervous movement, and Rabideau's fast breathing. Corelli's finger tightened about his rifle trigger, but still he held his fire.

The horses were nearer now. For a moment they paused. For an instant Corelli feared they might turn back. Then a soft breath of relief was expelled from his lips. The horses were moving on again, coming down the short slope that led to the water's edge. For a brief moment their forms blurred against the opposite bank, before the hoofs splashed through the water. Now, not ten yards away, the two mounted figures took shape before him in the gloom.

Abruptly, the animals halted in midstream to drink. Corelli could scarcely contain the exclamation of exultation that rose in his throat. A motionless target to fire at! This was even more than he had wished for.

"Give it to 'em!" Corelli snapped through clenched teeth.

His finger clenched savagely on trigger. A spurt of orange fire ripped the gloom. Beside him the crashing of his companions' rifles tore the silence wide open.

One of the mounted figures swayed back and sagged almost out of the saddle. The sudden splash of water beat triumphantly on Corelli's ears as the second figure toppled to the stream. He fired again and again!

Corelli could contain himself no longer. Leaping erect, he yelled, "C'mon, we'll pour in some forty-five lead to make this good—!"

And that was as far as he got. From the opposite bank there ran livid tongues of flaming lead. Something hot slashed violently into Corelli's body. White fire burst in his brain! He whirled twice around, then plunged in at the water's edge, his face submerged below the surface.

"God!" Kraft exclaimed. "What the—?" He swung to face the firing from the opposite bank, which by this time had been redoubled. Even as he moved, a leaden slug struck him, tearing through bone and flesh and muscle. Without a word he slumped down, the rifle falling from his suddenly weakened grasp.

A scream of fear was torn from Rabideau's lips. He crashed to earth with a bullet through his thigh. Even as he fell, a second leaden slug ripped across the top of his shoulder. He groveled low in the brush, his high-pitched voice begging: "Don't—don't! Don't shoot any more. Gawd! Give me a chance!"

Then Tucson Smith's voice from the opposite side of the stream: "You deserve about as much chance as you would have given us, coyote. All right, toss your gun away. We're coming across . . . Stony, cover me, until I see what we've trapped."

He came plunging down the slope and splashed across the stream, thigh deep. Cautiously, six-shooter in hand, he ploughed through the brush until he came to the moaning figure of Rabideau, sprawled face down, his clothing blood-stained.

With one hand, Tucson struck a match. Rabideau's rifle lay some feet away where he had thrown it. Tucson jerked out the man's Colt gun and flung it into the stream. His gaze strayed farther as he struck a second match. Kraft lay motionless a few feet from Rabideau.

Tucson raised his voice. "Come across, Stony. Looks like this fracas is over."

Stony moved down the slope and splashed through the water. Emerging on the opposite side, he stumbled over the dead body of Snake Corelli. Tucson came down to the water's edge. "I thought there were three scuts shooting," he said. A third match was lighted. He glanced briefly at the silent figure. "Well, that's the end of Corelli. I think Kraft's finished as well. Rabideau's still alive."

The match flickered out. Leaving Corelli's body where it had fallen, they made their way back into the brush, water dripping from pant legs and boots. Stony twisted a small torch from some dried brush and twigs. It burned well when lighted. Kraft was dead, as Tucson had suspected. They turned Rabideau on his back. The man looked up at them, mingled fear and defiance in his eyes.

Tucson said grimly, "What do you think I should do with you, Rabideau?"

"That's up to you, Smith," Rabideau said doggedly. "I ain't begging for mercy—and if I get another chance at you I'm hoping for better luck."

Tucson laughed softly. "Right or wrong, Rabideau, I'll hand it to you. You got nerve. I can't kill a game man, no matter how much he deserves it."

"Don't give me any of that palaver, Smith," Rabideau sneered. "I'm not aiming to change sides. Bronc Rabideau doesn't take one man's money and then bargain with another."

"There's no bargaining necessary," Tucson said tersely. "We know Nirvan sent you three out to drop us. Am I right?"

"You tell me," Rabideau retorted sullenly. "I'm not talking. But so long as you're not gunning me, I'll give you a friendly hint. Clear out of this country as fast as your horses will carry you. No man can buck Matt Nirvan and live."

"We seem to be doing it," Stony put in.

"Yaah!" Rabideau spat angrily. "We got two hombres anyway. If we'd known there was four of you coming, we'd been ready—"

Tucson laughed shortly. "What two you referring to, Rabideau?"

"Those two we pumped full of lead—them that started across the stream. We thought it was you and Brooke, but maybe it was Joslin and—who else?—Johnny Jump-Up?"

Stony chuckled. "You mean the pair on the horses? They were just our old friends, Beans and Bacon. We named 'em on the way here."

"Talk sense, will you?" Rabideau protested through his pain.

Tucson explained, "Beans and Bacon were just

two dummies Stony and I fixed up on our way. I sort of had a hunch somebody might be waiting for us here, it's such a fine place for an ambush, so we sort of prepared—"

"Tucson Smith, you're a devil!" Rabideau burst out. He came to a sitting position, then sank back as sudden pain gripped him.

"Damned if he didn't faint," Stony exclaimed. "What'll we do with him, Tucson?"

"Fix him up as best as possible," Tucson said reluctantly.

Stony built a small fire of twigs and dried cactus pads, which furnished light to work by. They made a quick examination of Rabideau and found his wounds not too serious. A slug had ploughed an ugly furrow across his collarbone, and the bullet had struck his thigh and gone clear through without touching bone. With Rabideau's bandanna, and handkerchiefs taken from the clothing of Corelli and Kraft, Tucson managed to bandage the wounds and stop the flow of blood. A flask of whiskey was found in Kraft's pocket and a couple of stiff drinks poured down Rabideau's throat brought him to his feet. He swayed a moment but managed to retain his balance.

Tucson brought up the three horses of the gunmen. The dead bodies were lashed in place with lariats on the saddles. Stony said, "Think you should put your X brand on Kraft?"

"I already slashed Corelli proper," Tucson said

grimly, "but I can't continue such Injun type mutilation as a steady diet. We'll leave that sort of thing for Nirvan and his coyotes."

Bronc Rabideau, leaning against his horse, shoulder and leg bandaged, looked his relief at Tucson's words. He sneered through white lips, "That's the reason you stand to lose out against Matt Nirvan, Smith. You're too chicken-hearted."

"Yes?" Tucson smiled thinly. Drawing his six-shooter he thrust one finger into the end of the barrel. It came out covered with black powder soot. With the end of his blackened finger, Tucson drew an X on the dead Kraft's forehead.

"Rabideau," he said, "I've already branded you with my lead. This brand mark on Kraft is to show Nirvan he has a strong brand bucking him. In algebra, X stands for unknown quantity. So far as Nirvan knows, my pards and I are an unknown quantity, and maybe Nirvan will learn that we figure out to more than three before we're through."

"Aw, hell," Rabideau growled, "let's cut out the *habla*, and get started with whatever you plan to do with me. If you figure on putting me in jail—"

"Jail?" Tucson said scornfully. "That would be wasted effort. No, Rabideau, I'm going to let you go. You can return these bodies to Nirvan with my regards. Tell him we're just getting started. We're not asking for a truce and we're not giving any."

"You'll be wishing for more than a truce," Rabideau snarled.

"Come on," Tucson said impatiently, "I'll give you a boost into your saddle, Rabideau. You've had your chance. If you don't get back to town all right, it's your own fault."

He led the three horses across the stream, two with the dead bodies lashed face down across saddles. Then placing the lead reins in Rabideau's hand he said shortly, "Get going." Rabideau's face was twisted with pain. He stared down at Tucson. Tucson handed him Kraft's whiskey flask. "Take a swig of this now and then, Rabideau. You'll make it all right, I reckon."

"Aw, go to hell," Rabideau mumbled defiantly. He jabbed spurs into his horse, and the three animals moved off, quickly melting into the darkness.

Tucson returned to Stony's side. Stony said, "I've got a hunch we'd been better off if we'd finished that coyote."

"Could be you're right as hell," Tucson answered soberly. "But you wouldn't do it while he's down and neither would I. If we'd tied him up someplace he'd be a nuisance to take care of. Anyway I sent him back for the psychological effect on Nirvan—"

"Socko-what? How you aiming to sock Nirvan?"

"By making him understand we don't have to

kill a man when we could. That rubbing out a scut like Rabideau is too small a matter for us to bother with—come on, let's get our horses."

They found the animals just a short way down stream, nibbling at brush-tips. One of the animals still carried on its back a dummy. "This must be Bacon," Stony said, unlashing the dummy. "It's got your Stet-hat on. Beans has got my hat, and he fell off. Now where in the devil could he have floated to?"

Fortunately, they found "Beans," but a short distance farther on, where "he" had been snagged by an overhanging root at the water's edge. Stony donned his sombrero and they headed back to their mounts.

"We'd better move at a right smart clip," Tucson said. "It's after midnight now. I'd sure like to wait until morning to hit the Wagon-Wheel and break the bad news, but we'd best push on. I hope I can see that foreman first. He knows the girl and can like's not make a better job of it."

The two men mounted, spoke to their horses and shoved on toward the Wagon-Wheel.

IX

Matt Nirvan gleefully rubbed his long thin hands together, pulled out a drawer in his desk and produced a box of cigars. He picked out one of the weeds, then passed the box to Santone; Black Payette, Shive Otis and Riker Wetzel also sat in his office.

Wetzel said, when they'd lighted up, "You're feeling right good, Matt."

"Why not?" Nirvan chuckled wickedly. "Things are coming my way. Those fool cowhands didn't have any more sense than to split forces, which makes things easier for us. It won't be long now before Corelli and the other two will be drifting back with word that Smith and Brooke won't cause any more trouble."

"Could be," Santone conceded. "Just the same, Matt, it ain't wise to count your cows before they're branded."

"Bosh! Smith and Brooke won't have a chance against our boys hid and waiting in the brush. Quit fretting, Santone."

"Like's not you're correct, Matt," Wetzel nodded. "How you going to handle Joslin?"

"We'll get him and Johnny at the same time. I'm waiting for Pete to report back from the Brown Bottle now—" At that moment Pete's arrival was announced by a knock on the door. He came in and closed the door at his back. Nirvan said, “Brown Bottle closed?”

“Twenty minutes back,” Pete said.

“Why didn’t you let me know sooner?” Nirvan demanded.

Pete’s gaze shifted uneasily. “I figured I’d better wait to make sure of things. I snuck around to the back of the Brown Bottle and waited. Pretty soon the lights were put out. I heard Joslin and Johnny heading for the cots in that back room. They talked a few minutes, then the snoring started—from both of ’em. It’ll be their first sleep, Mister Nirvan. They won’t be woke up easy. The streets are dark. There’s only a few hombres paradin’ around.”

“Good!” Nirvan exclaimed. “Good, Pete. You’re a credit to my training.”

Black Payette looked interested. “Matt, if you’re figuring to have a couple of guns pushed through that back window, count me in.”

Nirvan shook his head. “No gunwork. No use letting the town learn too much too early. This is a job for knives as I see it. Shive, I can use you—and you’ll get the usual bonus.”

“I’m ready, Matt,” Otis nodded.

Nirvan pondered a moment. “Pete, you claimed to be right good with a knife at one time, before the booze trapped you. If your hand was steady enough—”

"It's steady," Pete cut in, new life coming to his dull eyes. "If you'll remember, I showed Shive a trick or two he didn't know."

"That's true enough," Otis admitted grudgingly.

"Fine," Nirvan said. "Pete, it's about time I let you have a real job. You'll go with Shive. Now listen close." He puffed deeply on his cigar for a moment, then, "Pete and Shive will get some old rags and soak 'em in oil, so they'll burn easy. Then both of you go to the Brown Bottle. Pete, you take some of them oil-soaked rags and push them through that small barred window at the right of the entrance. It's never closed. Meanwhile, Shive can be piling more oiled rags at the back wall of the building. But don't light 'em right away, Shive—"

"You're forgetting something, Matt," Black Payette broke in. "The Brown Bottle being built of adobe won't catch fire easy, if you're figuring to burn those two hombres up while they're asleep. They might wake up and get out."

"All right, Blackie," Nirvan said patiently. "That's a good point. But the wood inside will burn and that's all that's necessary right now. Wait until you hear me out." He went on, "After Pete has dropped his oily rags inside the front window, he strikes a match and drops it on the rags. There'll be an immediate flare-up. Then Pete runs around to the back door and wakes up Johnny and Joslin—tells 'em the place is burning down. They'll get up and see the flames in the barroom. Being half asleep they won't be thinking fast and—"

"I get it," Wetzel broke in. "Johnny's well is back of his place. Him and Joslin will grab buckets and dash out there for water."

"That's the idea." Nirvan chuckled. "As they come running out, Shive and Pete throw the steel into them." He paused to let this statement sink in. "Shive, when that's done, drag the bodies inside. Then use more oily rags to help the whole place get going. Get back here as soon as possible, leaving the bodies to burn."

Payette said, "That's a smart stunt, Matt."

"It's slick," Nirvan agreed. "There'll be no shots to arouse the town. It'll look as though the building caught fire natural and those two couldn't escape the blaze. And for once Matt Nirvan won't be suspected of murder. This all okay with you and Pete, Shive?"

"Suits me fine," Otis replied.

Pete hesitated. "The plan's all right, but what do I get out of it, Mister Nirvan? I figure I deserve more than a couple of silver dollars."

"Don't worry about your pay," Nirvan laughed. "I'll take care of you, Pete. You'll be able to get some new togs and still have enough for whiskey and the girls. Suit you?"

"I can't kick, Mister Nirvan."

"Fine, Pete. You won't be sorry. There's one

thing more. Riker"—to Wetzel—"go out and announce that the Purgatoire is closing early tonight. We'll get everybody out and give them time to get to their beds. We need the street empty while Shive and Pete work. We're always the last to close, so it shouldn't be long before the streets are completely deserted."

Riker went to carry out Nirvan's order. Within a short time the hum of activity beyond the office door came to a stop. Fifteen minutes later, Wetzel returned, bearing a canvas sack containing the evening's receipts. He dropped the sack on the desk. "I didn't take time to count it, Matt. Everybody's left and the gals and the barkeep has gone upstairs to their beds. I closed the front doors, but didn't have the keys to lock 'em."

Nirvan said, "I'll go out later and lock up. We'll wait for Shive and Pete to come back and report."

Only the light from the stars shone along the deserted street when Shive Otis and Pete stepped out, three quarters of an hour later. No one was in sight, though from the Mexican quarter, south of town, there came on the night breeze the faint strumming of guitar music. The buildings on both sides of the street were dark. Otis and Pete moved boldly along. Once, Pete started nervously as something stirred between buildings.

Otis laughed scornfully. "Buck up, Pete. That was just a stray cur." Pete swore as the animal tagged after them a few minutes then again lost itself in the shadows. The two moved swiftly on, each bearing in his hand a big bundle of oil-soaked rags.

At the Brown Bottle they came to a stop and glanced quickly both ways along the deserted street. From somewhere in the rear of the building came loud snoring noises. "They're dead to the world," Otis whispered. "Get busy on your job, Pete. I'll drift around to the back and wait, until you bring me word you've got your fire lit. Then we'll wake up those dumb sons and finish our work."

With a last nod to his companion, Otis moved stealthily around to the back of the building, proceeding through a passageway that separated the Brown Bottle from a gunsmith's shop. Here he faded into the shadows, waiting.

Pete scuffled to the porch of the Brown Bottle. Through the small wooden-barred window to the right of the doorway, he peered inside the saloon. The interior was dark. There wasn't a thing to be seen. The snoring from the back of the building now sounded louder. Pete shook his head. "Them hombres sure can sleep."

Everything was going according to schedule. Within a short time the Brown Bottle could be transformed to a roaring inferno, once the work got under way. Pete started pushing oily rags through the bars of the window. That done, he reached for a match. It crackled loudly in the silence and flared into a small flame. Holding the lighted match to the bars, Pete tried to peer within to determine where the rags had fallen. It came to him suddenly it might have been better to have set fire to the rags first, before shoving them within. Still they might have stuck between the bars and he could have scorched his fingers.

While he stood there, thinking about it, the match flickered out. Pete cursed in an undertone, groped in his pocket for a second match. He found it, scratched it across the wall. It burst into instant flame.

Raising it to the bars, he paused abruptly, as something round and hard was pressed against his spine. It wasn't necessary to think twice to realize the "something" was the end of a gun barrel. Then came a cool, drawly voice:

"I wouldn't try that hombre, was I you. You might get your fingers burned. So drop it—damn fast!"

X

“Drop it—damn fast!”

In the silence of the night the words reached clearly to Shive Otis, waiting at the rear of the building. Otis tensed, took one step forward to go to Pete’s assistance, then changed his mind. It would be better to stay hidden where he was. Whoever it was who had caught Pete, would be on the alert for anyone else.

Otis caught Pete’s sharp cry of alarm. “Don’t shoot, Joslin. I didn’t mean no harm to anybody.”

Shive Otis stiffened. Joslin? Hell, Joslin was supposed to be asleep inside with Johnny Jump-Up. Pete must be mistaken. Through the turmoil of thought racing through Otis’s mind came the snoring of a single man from the rear of the building. That must be Johnny. It was Joslin out front, all right.

Otis cursed softly under his breath, straining his ears for further words. For a time they were indistinct, then as Pete’s fright increased he talked louder:

“Lemme go, Mister Joslin. I reckon I was drunk and didn’t realize what I was doing. I got sort of mad at Johnny one time, and every time I have a drop too much I get to thinking about—”

“Liar!” Joslin’s voice.

"I'm talkin' truth, Mister Joslin."

"Who's with you, Pete?"

"I don't understand what you mean."

"Now you're a liar on two counts. You understand all right. I know damn well you wouldn't be trusted alone to do a job like this. Who came with you? Anybody hiding around at the back?"

"Certain not. I ain't got any friends in this town. Look, Mister Joslin, I got to drinking and then I got mad and I come here alone. I'm just a plain damn' fool. Let me go and I'll—"

"Maybe you're telling truth at that," Otis heard Joslin reply. "But I reckon I'll go around back and see for myself."

Otis couldn't catch Pete's answer. From within the building came Johnny's sleepy tones, "Did you call me, Lullaby?" The words weren't loud enough to carry far. Lullaby didn't hear them. The cot creaked as Johnny rolled over and continued to mumble thickly in a half-waking doze. Otis caught Lullaby's voice again:

"Yep, I'll drift around back and see if you've been telling the truth—"

There came the sound of a scuffle as Pete tried to break away. Then a dull *thwack,* followed by a groan.

Otis knew what that meant; he'd heard it many times before. Joslin had struck Pete over the head with his gun barrel. Then came the sound of Joslin's voice again, "Maybe you'd better wait for me here, Pete."

There was no reply.

A feeling of triumph ran through Otis. This was a piece of luck. He'd be able to get Joslin, anyway, and, perhaps, Johnny Jump-Up later. Otis turned and moved back to a high pile of rubbish, empty bottles and tin cans heaped a few yards to the rear of the Brown Bottle, deep in shadow. Here he drew his knife, experimentally ran one thumb nail along the keen-edged blade, and crouched, waiting for Lullaby Joslin to appear.

There was silence out in front of the Brown Bottle. Then Joslin's voice. "I reckon that will hold you for a spell, Pete. Now I'll just mosey along to the back of this building and see how things stand."

Otis tensed as slow footsteps moved around the side of the building. A moment more and Joslin would be within knife range. Otis straightened up, knife balanced in right hand, arm far back for the deadly throw.

The footsteps came nearer. Evidently Joslin was moving with caution. He wasn't hurrying. Otis quivered with excitement. His hand, holding the knife, tingled. Only a few more steps now and Joslin would be in sight. Then would come the death-dealing flash of the sharpened steel blade.

A dark figure edged slowly around the rear corner of the building, taking definite shape in the gloom. Otis hesitated but a moment longer, eyes straining to discern outlines, gauging distance, so he could make his throw to a vital point. Then he made out the high crown of Joslin's sombrero. Good! Now he had the range.

With the deadly speed of a striking diamond-back, Otis's arm snapped forward. There came the momentary gleam of bluish razor-keen blade as the knife winged viciously through the night. Then a soft thud!

Otis waited only a second. He *knew* his blade had found the throat, piercing the jugular vein. There came a strangled choking sound, a sharp agonized cry, as the shadowy form of the victim staggered back, disappearing around the corner of the building. Then the crashing down of a falling body.

From within the building came plaintive words from Johnny, words thick with sleep: "Did you say something, Lullaby?"

But Lullaby didn't reply.

Now Otis heard Johnny rising from his cot. His knife gone, he'd have to depend on his gun to finish Johnny. But Nirvan had said he didn't want guns used. It would be best to clear out as soon as possible, before Johnny emerged from the rear door.

Otis backed away, turned stealthily and ran swiftly through the night. Once, as he left, he thought he heard something from the man he'd downed, but he couldn't be certain, as he slipped speedily along the alleyway back of the buildings. He was moving so fast he passed the rear of the Purgatoire before he realized it. Discovering his error, he paused, cut through a passageway between a store and a saloon and emerged on the street. Quickly he turned back to the Purgatoire, ascended the broad steps that fronted the building and pushed through the dimly lighted empty barroom and dance hall.

The big room was deserted, but a brighter sliver of light shone through the crack beneath Nirvan's closed office door. From within came the sounds of droning voices. Without stopping to knock, Otis plunged inside, slamming the door at his rear. Panting heavily from his run, he slumped weakly into a chair.

"What the hell!" Nirvan exclaimed.

" 'S'all right," Otis gasped. "I got Joslin! Tell—story—when I catch—my breath."

"Good, by God!" Elatedly, Nirvan's clenched fist struck the desk.

Santone rose and poured a drink for Otis. The man gulped, strangled, coughed. Black Payette and Riker Wetzel both reached for the bottle and, grinning, poured drinks. Otis's voice was coming in wheezy gasps. "Not hurt, are you?" Nirvan asked.

Otis shook his head. "Tell you—in a minute—"

"Where's Pete?" Payette asked.

"Tell—in a—few minutes—"

They waited impatiently.

Otis smiled sheepishly at last. "I was sure—bushed. Ain't run so fast in a year?"

"What were you running from?" Nirvan demanded.

" 'Fraid Johnny would see me. I'd thrun my knife and you said not to use a gun."

"Didn't you get Johnny? Is the place burning?" Nirvan asked.

Otis shook his head to both questions. "Just—got Joslin. It went like this, Matt. Me and Pete went to the Brown Bottle. I left Pete at the front to do his job and went around to the back. Heard Pete strike a couple of matches, then Joslin's voice. Joslin wasn't asleep a-tall. Joslin must have thrun his gun on Pete, 'cause I heard Pete beggin' for mercy. But Pete didn't tell him I was at the back. Joslin decides to look for himself, and he cracked Pete over the head with his gun. Then like a damn' fool he comes walking around to the back. With that I slung my knife the minute he showed up. I didn't miss. I saw him stagger back and heard his carcass hit the ground—"

"You're sure you got Joslin?" Nirvan asked eagerly.

Otis said with pride, "Certain. I couldn't miss at that distance. Right through the throat he got it. I've heard my knife strike a mark like that before, and I didn't make any mistake."

"Good work, Shive," Nirvan said.

"I'll bet Joslin's blood spurted a mile when my blade slashed in. Hate to lose that knife too, but Johnny was getting up and I figured I'd best not stop to get it, so—"

"I'll buy you a dozen knives," Nirvan beamed. "I suppose Pete is still dead to the world in front of the Brown Bottle—"

"I reckon. Want one of us to go get him?"

Nirvan shook his head. "He'll come around by himself. Well, we'll just have to get Johnny another time—wait!"—struck by a sudden idea—"I wonder if we could hang Joslin's murder on Johnny. I'll have to think about that."

The room burst into laughter. Nirvan chuckled. "I can't think of a better joke. I believe I'll fix it up. I'll have Yarrow arrest Johnny for the killing, then we'll try Johnny all legal—after planting some solid evidence against him. Shive, didn't Johnny borrow that knife of yours one time and never return it?"

"He sure did if you say so, Matt," Otis laughed.

Nirvan seized the bottle. "I think we'd best have a drink all around on the killing and Johnny Jump-Up's coming trial."

When the drinks had been downed, Payette said, "What are we going to do about Pete?"

Nirvan shrugged. "He's probably come awake by this time and sneaked off some place to sleep. He won't want to face me after the way he let himself get caught. If anybody does find him there, we can always claim he had a part in Joslin's death, too. You boys heard him admit he took money from Johnny—"

"Somebody might break Pete down, make him talk," Santone suggested.

"We can have him quiet for good," Nirvan said carelessly, "if he opens his mouth too wide."

By this time the men were beginning to feel the effects of the liquor they'd taken. Practically anything said now produced a laugh. The world was a very funny place at the moment and every one was feeling in the best of humor.

Consequently, no one noticed it when the doorknob of the office door turned slightly. Then it turned a trifle farther. . . .

"Say," Black Payette asked, "ain't it about time that Corelli and Kraft and Rabideau got back with some more good news?"

"Just about," Nirvan nodded. "Christ! What a night's work. We get rid of Smith, Brooke and Joslin, all in the space of a few hours. Boys, we'll sure have to celebrate. When Corelli and the other two get back I'm going to break out a couple bottles of rare old stuff I've been saving for just such an occasion. Yes, sir, I aim to break out—"

Crash! The door burst violently open, smashing against the inner wall, under the impact of a heavy, booted foot!

"You're going to break out with a rash from your own venom, Nirvan, I'm betting," came a cool intrusive voice.

There, framed in the open doorway stood Lullaby Joslin, a leveled six-shooter in his right hand. Slung over his left shoulder was the dead body of Pete, a knife blade buried to the hilt in Pete's throat.

XI

There ensued a sudden stunned silence, broken only by the slow dropping of blood as it struck the planks of the office floor. Abruptly, chairs banged back and Nirvan and his henchmen leaped to their feet, hands starting toward holsters.

"Hold it!" Lullaby said sharply, gun swinging in a slow arc that seemed to cover every man in the room.

The men hesitated, midway in their draws, then slowly relaxed and stared angrily at the intruder, each one fighting to hold his temper and not daring to draw in the face of such opposition.

Lullaby's next tones were easier. "That's fine. I can see you're gents of discretion. Now—one at a time—draw your guns if you like, but don't try to pull triggers. Just toss those hawg-laigs of yours over in that far corner."

"I'm damned if I will!" Nirvan exploded.

"You'll be worse damned if you don't," Lullaby said placidly. "And the same goes for all of you. Now do as I tell you or take the consequences. I'm sick of taking anything more from you scuts, so get busy. Last man to hit that corner with his gun is due to—"

There came a sudden eager rush to dispose of

weapons. Six-shooters went clattering across the plank floor.

"—is due to," Lullaby finished, "be called a monkey's uncle." He snickered. "Sort of stampeded for a few minutes there, didn't you, gents? You're lucky the shock didn't set off any of those guns when they landed. I'd sure hate to see any slugs flying wild while I'm around here. It might have made me nervous and I'd start rolling lead too. But I reckon to give you all high marks for prompt attention. All except Mister Nirvan. He's trying to play hide-and-seek with me. If you're not seeking trouble, Nirvan, you'd better dispose of that hideout gun under your coat. And I don't want to tell you twice."

Cursing, Nirvan ripped back his coat lapel and produced a small caliber weapon which he sent to join the others.

"Ace-in-the-hole, eh, Nirvan," Lullaby said genially. "Well, you get an A for effort on that one. Now, if you gents will just stand back a moment I'll unload my burden."

A slight lifting of his gun barrel resulted in fast steps away from the desk. Still keeping Nirvan and his henchmen covered, Lullaby moved forward with the dead Pete balanced on his shoulder like a sack of flour. Nearing the desk, he jerked the left shoulder forward and the body fell across the desk-top, face upward, dead eyes glazed. Crimson drops spattered the desk.

Nirvan paled. Otis's jaw dropped. Lullaby laughed softly, "And all the time you thought it was me got pig-stuck."

"I—I—I—" Otis stammered.

"We don't know what you're talking about, Joslin," Nirvan cut in. "What you bringing that dead no-good here for? This is no undertaker's establishment."

"I insist that it is," Lullaby drawled. "Only you undertook more than you could handle."

Santone burst out, "I'm damned if I can understand—" then abruptly checked the words, realizing he was saying too much.

Lullaby grinned at the break. He nodded toward Santone. "Curiosity's the greatest thing in the world, gents. Think where science would be without it. Now, this little matter, and I know you're all plumb curious, can be cleared up in a minute. I figured this Pete hombre might be up to skulduggery when I saw him hanging around the Brown Bottle, before Johnny closed up. Anyway, after we turned in, Johnny snored so loud I couldn't sleep. Just for fun I made snoring sounds louder than his, trying to wake him up, but, shucks! it wasn't any use."

Lullaby paused, grinning at the strained expression on Nirvan's face. "What's wrong? Did Pete tell you two men were snoring? Well, don't hold it against him. We all make mistakes. Anyway, I got up and went for a walk. Being a lazy sort of cuss I sat down to rest in the shadows across from the Brown Bottle. Before long I saw Pete and this other hombre approaching the Brown Bottle. This knife-slinging scut goes around to the back. Pete stays on the porch and starts playing with matches—"

"It wasn't me with Pete," Otis blurted.

"You're a liar," Lullaby said quietly. "Well, I was afraid Pete might burn himself so I crossed over to stop him. We had some *habla*, but he got difficult. So I persuaded him with a little tap of my gun barrel."

Lullaby paused long enough to step toward the desk and pick a smoke from Nirvan's open box of cigars. Deliberately he bit off one end, spat it out and reached for a match. All the time his gun muzzle was moving in the same slow arc, back and forth, covering everyone in the room. He struck the match and lighted up, then stepped back. Cigar smoke drifted from his lips.

"Good cigar, Nirvan," he complimented. "Sometimes you show fine judgment."

"Go to hell!" Nirvan glowered.

"Naughty, naughty," Lullaby chided insolently. "Mustn't use swear words. Mama will have to wash out your mouth with alcohol."

"If you got anything to say, say it and get out," Nirvan said furiously.

Lullaby nodded. "So I'll get on with my story. Anyway, I had a feeling that somebody was waiting at the back of the Brown Bottle, so I sent Pete first. That little tap on the head I'd handed him wasn't enough to knock him cold. It just made him a mite groggy, and he didn't know what was happening from then on, as I pushed him ahead of me. Just to make things more involvicated—ain't that a nice word, Nirvan?—just to make things more involvicated for the hidden assassin who skulked in darkness waiting to lay me low—I heard that at the opera house one time—I stuck my Stet hat on poor Pete, never dreamin' that he was due to become a victim of mistaken identity—"

A sudden exclamation from Otis interrupted.

Lullaby gave him a short bow. "Yes, that's it. The mystery of the twin identities is solved. Pete didn't turn out to be my grandfather, after all. Nor was I his'n. He was Pete—alas, a deceased Pete, pierced through and through by the villainous blade of a scoundrelly knave—"

"God damn it!" Nirvan exclaimed furiously. "Cut out this foolishness—"

"There's already been too much cutting for one night," Lullaby reproved. "Well, when Pete dropped I didn't realize he'd been stuck. Figured he was just dizzy from the wallop I gave him. I stooped to pick him up again—and then, alas, too late, the galloping hoofprints of the departing butcher were wafted to my ears. Maybe I should have took after him, but it wasn't me that had been hurt. Nirvan, your little pals sure play rough—"

"I tell you we don't know anything—"

"I already realized that. But I'm asking you, please and polite like, don't leave any more messes like that around the Brown Bottle. Johnny likes to keep his place neat. Well, that's all. I reckon now to saunter back to the arms of Morpheus. Just a word of advice. Don't be in a rush to come after me. I'm in no mood to have company on my walk. So wait here and meditate on your sins, and nothing will happen to you."

Laughing, he backed swiftly to the doorway, seized the doorknob, stepped out to the barroom and slammed the door after him.

Instantly, Nirvan and the others rushed to get their guns, bumping into each other in the scramble. They didn't lose time opening the door but cut loose in the general direction of Lullaby's departure. The office shook with the heavy detonations of six-shooters, as slug after slug ripped through the door panels. The room filled with powder smoke. Coughing, Nirvan called for the shooting to stop. The men listened intently. There wasn't a sound to be heard from the big outer room. Nirvan said, "Wetzel, open the door."

Wetzel looked uneasy. "Maybe we'd better wait a few minutes, Matt. That Joslin might be waiting for us. Can't tell what to expect from a feller as crazy as he is. He just don't know enough to be afraid. He's just plain *loco!*"

Otis said, "I haven't heard any groans, or anything—"

"*You* wouldn't," Nirvan snapped. "You can't see straight, either."

Otis flushed. "How the hell was I to tell in the dark—"

"You messed up the whole job," Nirvan snarled. "Don't try to tell me different. Wetzel, open that door. Have your gun ready. If you see Joslin on the floor, pour more lead into him. Some of our shots must have hit him."

Cautiously, Wetzel opened the door a few inches.

Wham! Wham! Two leaden slugs splintered the doorjamb. Wetzel slammed shut the door with frantic violence. He turned white-faced to his chief. Nirvan said dumbly, "He—he must be still there." The others were cursing in frustration.

"Yeah, he's there," Wetzel nodded. "Standing behind the bar, helping himself to a drink." There was a certain awe in the man's tones.

From the big barroom came Lullaby's laughing voice. "Your liquor's not bad either, Nirvan. Take my advice and don't open that door again. I like to drink in peace, and that's right hard to do with a gun in my hand."

Lullaby finished his drink, then softly left the building.

Within the office, Nirvan and his men gave

themselves over to futile cursing. From above came the sounds of frightened girls' voices. Nirvan roared at them to shut up and go back to sleep. The voices stopped. Nirvan started to speak, choked, glaring at the others. No one had anything to offer. There was nothing to do but wait until such time as they were certain Lullaby had departed. The minutes dragged on, passed to quarter hours.

Suddenly, running steps were heard outside, then Trent Volpone's voice: "Matt! Matt! Are you in there?" An instant later the deputy plunged into the room. His hair was tousled, his nightshirt tucked into his pants. He had no hat but the holster was strapped about his hips. "Wha—what's up?" he stammered.

"Didn't you hear the shots?" Nirvan demanded angrily.

"Sure, I heard some shooting, but knew you had some plans afoot, so figured we'd best keep out of things until you sent for us. Then Joslin woke up Beef and me and told us there'd been some shooting here and you wanted me right away. Beef will be here in a minute—"

"Joslin woke you up?" Nirvan fairly exploded.

"Yeah—Joslin. He said there was a dead man here. I figured it must be Smith or Brooke—"

"That damn cowhand! S'help me, before I get through with him, he'll know better than to play jokes—"

Nirvan stiffened suddenly, staring wide-eyed beyond Volpone's shoulder, through the open door of the office.

Bronc Rabideau, his gait lurching, was making an unsteady way across the big room, so weak he could scarcely walk. His shoulder and one pant leg were stained darkly. All the blood seemed drained from his features. He staggered into the office and half fell across the body of the dead Pete.

"Christ A'mighty! What now?" Nirvan cursed. Leaping to the wounded gunman's side, he seized him by the hair and twisted his face around. "Bronc! Speak to me! What's happened? Where's Corelli? And Gage Kraft?"

Rabideau slowly opened his eyes. "Deader'n door-nails, Matt," he mumbled thickly. "I brought 'em in on their ponies—out at hitchrack. That devil—Smith—outfoxed us."

Nirvan broke into a fit of cursing that drove the rest to the barroom, while Nirvan raged like a maniac. After a time, Santone and Wetzel summoned enough courage to go in and care for the unconscious Rabideau who had by now slipped to the floor.

XII

It must have been one in the morning when Tucson and Stony reached the Wagon-Wheel Ranch. The trail wasn't difficult to follow as it wound through mesquite and sage and cactus, finally straightening out to run an almost direct course across rolling grasslands. Finally, through the night, they caught sight of several small rectangles of yellow light. They spoke to their ponies and drew closer. In time the blocky outlines of buildings took form, and the steady clanking of a windmill was heard through the gloom.

Tucson noticed a light in the ranch house as they rode down past the building on the way to the corrals and bunkhouse, their horses now pulled to a slower gait. "Looks to me," Tucson commented, "like that girl is waiting up for her pa. Poor kid."

"It's a tough break," Stony said.

They had nearly reached the bunkhouse when the door was flung open. The yellow light beyond silhouetted a tall spare figure in the doorway. A voice, tinged with anxiety, reached them. "That you, Sam?"

"No, it's not, pardner. We're strangers to you."

Before he could say more the back door of the ranch house was flung open. The tall man in the bunkhouse doorway called quickly, "It ain't yore paw, Louise. Couple of punchers dropped in to say hello."

"All right, Ringbone," came the girl's answer and her door closed again.

Three other figures joined the one in the bunkhouse doorway. The tall man spoke, " 'Light, strangers, and come on in. If you can stay the night, just turn your hawsses into the saddlers' corral. If you'll hold up a minute I'll get a lantern and show you the way."

"We'll stay, thanks," Tucson replied. "We're looking for Ringbone Tilford."

"That's me. Be with you in a minute."

Tucson and Stony dismounted, waiting. Within a few minutes Tilford returned, carrying a lighted lantern. In its faint illumination, Tucson judged Tilford to be fifty-five or sixty. His skin was the texture of well-worn leather and his long mustaches were bleached to a creamy white. A typical cowman of the old school with knotted brown hands, frosty blue eyes and a long easy stride.

"You say you was looking for me?" Tilford asked, when the ponies had been turned into the corral, after being unsaddled.

Tucson nodded. "Johnny Jump-Up give us your name. I'm Tucson Smith. My pardner, here, is Stony Brooke." The men shook hands. Tucson and Stony lifted their saddles and trappings to the top bar of the pole corral, and waited for Tilford to continue.

Tilford said slowly at last. "I don't know why, exactly, but I've got a feeling yo're bringin' some sort of news 'bout Sam Dixon. He ain't come home, and if it's that sort of news yo're bringin', there ain't no need to break it gentle."

"I sure hate to say it, Tilford," Tucson said awkwardly, "but it's that kind of news. Sam Dixon is dead."

Tilford didn't speak for a moment. One hand opened and shut convulsively. His eyes looked moist in the light from the lantern. Twice he opened his mouth to speak and closed it again without uttering a sound. The words when they came were husky. "I had a hunch along those lines. Early this mawnin'—it's yesterday mawnin' by this time—a rider we'd never seen before stopped to tell us he'd seen three Wagon-Wheel steers in the chaparral, over in Twisted Gulch, near the Alamos River. There's some *loco* weed grows over that way, so we figured to get 'em out—"

"That's where we found the body," Stony put in. "Tucson and me and our other pard, Lullaby Joslin."

Tilford continued, "All the boys were out on the range. I wanted to go, but Sam, he allowed as he'd ride over there, turn the animals back to our range and then go on to Manzanita to settle his account at the general store. By evenin', we got to thinkin' it was odd he didn't get back, but occasional he stays in town. Still, I been sort of fretted about it. So's Sam's daughter." He swallowed hard and fell silent.

Tucson told how they had found the body and of the red slash on the forehead.

"I suspected as much," Tilford said grimly. " 'Course that talk of stray steers was just a lure to draw Sam into Twisted Gulch. Damn them murderin' coyotes, I'll—"

"If it'll make you feel any better, Tilford, I'm glad to tell you we've got the killers that murdered Mr. Dixon. Leastwise, we've got two prime suspects in the Manzanita jail. I don't think there's any doubt."

"That right? For sartain?" A different note came into the old cowman's voice, then his manner drooped again. " 'Less'n somethin's done mighty fast, them two won't be in jail long—not if Nirvan has his way. Who killed Sam? I want the story—no, wait, c'mon to the bunkhouse. The boys will want to know too."

In the bunkhouse, a long narrow building with bunks along one side and a table running down the center of the room, Tucson and Stony were introduced to three cowhands and a cook known as Sloppy Wuther. Sloppy was crippled with rheumatism and an ingrown disposition, but proved to be an excellent cook.

Curly Folsom, King Cole and Posthole Turner were the names of the three cowpunchers. Folsom and Cole were likable young fellows with lean bronzed jaws and fun-loving eyes. Posthole Turner was older, stringy like rawhide, and taciturn.

Tucson and Stony shook hands with the four men. Sloppy Wuther went to a huge fireplace that nearly filled one end of the bunkhouse and commenced raking together some glowing embers, over which he hung a huge coffee pot. Then he turned and disappeared through a doorway that marked the boundary between kitchen and bunkhouse.

"Bring cups for the lot of us, Sloppy," Tilford called. "We'll all be needin' some strong java. Smith and Brooke brought some bad news." He turned up the flame of the oil lamp suspended above the table.

Posthole Turner looked up quickly. "Sam?"

Tilford nodded. "Murdered."

Curly Folsom and King Cole jerked erect from their bunks where they'd been seated. As one man they reached for their guns. Posthole Turner strode savagely across the room, yanked his gun and belt from a nail and commenced buckling them at his hips. "Hell, oh, hell," he was mumbling over and over.

Sloppy Wuther carried in cups, slammed them violently down on the table. "A hell of a time to be drinkin' coffee," he stated bitterly. "I'll get my old Sharps rifle and bore—"

"Take it easy, boys," Tilford admonished. "The killers are in the hoosegow and we can't do anything about that right now. Smith and his pards took care of them to the best of their ability." The others looked at Tucson and his pard for a long moment, then nodded, and they realized they'd found solid friends.

Over steaming cups of coffee, Tucson related how they had found the body and the details that followed, clear through to the branding of Corelli with Tucson's gunsight and the attempted ambush at the creek by Corelli and the other two gunmen.

"Cripes! That's something like it!" Folsom exclaimed enthusiastically. "But where'd you get the dummies, Smith?"

Tucson explained. "When Johnny Jump-Up gave us the lay of the land and told us how to get here, I figured that spot at Cottonwood Creek would make a likely place for an ambush, was anybody so inclined. Some hombre named Pete had been listening in on our talk so I got a mite suspicious. Before we left town we got a couple of horse blankets and horse-blanket size safety pins from the livery. When we'd rode nearly to the stream, we stopped and made the dummies, stuffing them with old brush and sticks. Then we lashed 'em into saddles; with our hats on 'em, they looked real lifelike in the dark. We pushed the horses on down to the creek, and followed on foot behind."

"Jeepers! You fellers use your heads," King Cole said.

"The way things have been going," Tucson smiled, "we have had to."

Ringbone Tilford said, "I want to meet this pardner of yours—Lullaby Joslin, you said his name was? I want to shake his hand and say thanks."

"I reckon you'll have plenty chance to do that," Tucson replied. "We're figuring to stick around until things clear up and accounts with Nirvan get squared. We left Lullaby behind tonight so Johnny would have someone with him, but once the three of us are together again, maybe we can make a move in the right direction."

"That's fine," Tilford said. He frowned. "Lord, I should be going up to tell Louise about—about Sam. I shore dread it. Smith, have you got any plans in mind?"

"I've been doing some thinking," Tucson admitted. "It's like this. We all know Nirvan is responsible for the skulduggery hereabouts, but nobody seems to have any proof. In addition he's got the backing of the sheriff and his deputy—two officers duly elected by the county—wait a minute, now. We know those two are tools of Nirvan's, but our hands are tied. They've got authority and we haven't. It's well enough to say that Nirvan put Yarrow in office. The fact remains that Nirvan was just smart enough to have the law on his side to cover his dirty work."

"But what can we do?" Tilford asked. "How can we stop Nirvan with a set-up like that? The man's a killer. When he can't get what he wants, he kills for it. He tried to buy the Wagon-Wheel. Sam said no. You see what's happened. Now I expect he'll produce a bill-of-sale and swear that Sam sold him the holdin's."

"That may have been his original plan," Tucson pointed out, "but I doubt he'll try that right away. Everybody knows that Venner and Wonch worked for Nirvan—though he denies it—and now that we've put the bee on those two scuts, Nirvan will go slow. He don't dare do anything too raw."

"His cow thieves will probably continue to steal from us, though," Cole said bitterly. "Cripes A'mighty! How I do wish I could catch a couple of his men at that job sometime—"

"There's more to fear than rustlin', I'm thinkin'," Posthole Turner said gloomily. "Nirvan wants this ranch. It will belong to Miss Louise now. I'm thinkin' we'd best keep a close guard on her."

"Posthole talks sense," Stony agreed.

The men's faces went grim at the thought. "We'll keep an eye on her," Tilford nodded. "Tucson, what was the idea you had in mind?"

"I'd like to see another sheriff elected—one that can be trusted."

"Can't be done. Not for some time anyway. The next election is some months away."

"I was afraid of that. Well, here's my next move, if we're going to do things with authority. Tilford, you know the men in this country who can be trusted. Who are they? We'll need at least a dozen whose honesty is unquestioned. Preferably men who want to beat Nirvan—men who have suffered losses at his hands. Can you find a dozen such?"

Tilford nodded. "And twice that. I take it you want men with guts. Lemme see, there's Rawlins of the Rockin'-R; Petrie, who runs the Forked-Lightning outfit; Tim Underwood of the Boxed-U. . . . Doc Armstrong, our doctor and coroner will want to be in on it too . . ." Tilford continued and named a dozen more men whose integrity he felt certain about.

"Good," Tucson said. "Can you have those men here by tomorrow night?"

"Just the minute you explain your plan, I'll send the boys riding to tell 'em. There's no use waiting until tomorrow. They can slip into Manzanita before daylight, and call on the various ranches next. Posthole, you and King and Curly go saddle yore broncs. Be ready to ride. You can hear Tucson's plan later."

The three cowhands rose and left the bunkhouse. For some minutes, Tucson spoke steadily and to the point. When he had concluded, Tilford looked dubious. "Do you think it can be done?"

"The chances are even," Tucson said. "Nirvan likes to do things with the law on his side. To get any place, we've got to do likewise."

"But who can we get to enforce the law, once we have the authority?" Tilford wanted to know.

"One of the first twelve men you've named," Tucson said.

Tilford shook his head. "I don't know," he said slowly. "None of the men I've named is exactly young. Willing enough, yes, but a mite cramped on the draw. Game, but not as fast as they once was—"

Stony cut in, "How about letting Tucson handle the job?"

"Aw, now, Stony—" Tucson started a protest.

"By Gawd, the very thing," Tilford exclaimed. "You've proved you can buck Nirvan. Yo're the man for the job, if you'd do it. Would you?"

Tucson nodded. "I'd take it in a minute, if your friends want me. You're forgetting, they don't know me."

"My word carries weight with those hombres," Tilford stated. "If I okay you, they'll take my word for it. I like yore methods, Tucson. You don't let grass grow under foot. What we've needed is somebody to organize us. Yep, that settles it. Yo're the man to clean up Manzanita."

"If your friends approve," Tucson said.

"Let me worry about that." Tilford stood up. "I've stalled long enough. I've got to go to the house and tell Louise what happened. Gawd, how I hate to do it. The gal had a hunch something was wrong. She pretends to be sitting up reading a book, but I know she's just waitin' for Sam to return—waitin'—just waitin'."

Tucson said sympathetically, "It's sure bad news for the young lady. Was Sam Dixon her only relative?"

"Just about, except for a second cousin she writes to back East. This cousin is attending a theological school back there, but expects to come out here in a year or so. But of course that would be too late to give her any comfort now." Tilford drew a long sigh of resignation. "It's got to be done so I might's well go up and tell her. I'll stop at the corral first and tell Posthole and the other boys where I want 'em to ride. You and Stony make yourselfs at home. If you get hungry have Sloppy fix you a bait. I'll see you later."

XIII

The following morning, Tucson and Stony met Louise Dixon. She shook hands quietly with the two men, thanking them for what they'd done on her father's behalf. Despite the girl's pale features and moist blue-gray eyes, they could see she was extremely lovely, with her blonde hair like corn-silk and slim boyish form. Her chin quivered a trifle as she spoke, but she managed to hold back tears.

Tilford had performed the introductions out back of the ranch house. Louise had talked a few minutes then turned to go in, pausing at the back door to say, "I want both of you, Mr. Smith and Mr. Brooke, to make your home at the Wagon-Wheel just as long as you care to stay."

"Thanks, Miss Dixon," Tucson replied. Stony just nodded dumbly.

When the girl had left, Tucson said to Tilford, "She's taking it game."

Tilford nodded. "Sam's own daughter," as though that explained everything.

"Gosh, she's pretty," Stony half mumbled, his eyes still fixed on the door past which Louise Dixon had disappeared.

"You're not the only man to think that," Tilford said. "Plenty of the boys hereabouts have wanted to run in double harness with Louise, but while she's friendly with everyone, she ain't took any fellers around here serious yet. The gal always did have good sense."

Tucson changed the subject. "What about the funeral for her father? Has she said anything about arrangements? I'll do anything I can. So will Stony. And we'll get hold of Lullaby too."

Tilford raised one gnarled hand and pointed to an ancient live oak tree that raised wide branches above the ranch-house roof. "Louise's maw is buried there," he said simply. "Sam always allowed as he wanted to be buried alongside her. We'll do it this afternoon, with just a few friends present. I'm going in to see the undertaker this morning and bring the body back."

"Right sudden, isn't it?" Stony said.

"That's what I told Louise, but the gal is sensible. She don't see no use keepin' the body three-four days in Manzanita. Posthole and the other boys will be driftin' in by noon-time, I expect. I'll be back with the wagon by three-thirty or four, and we'll get things finished. Sloppy Wuther allows as he wants to dig the grave. There's no sky-pilot in Manzanita, but Louise figures I can use her Bible and wrangle out a service that will be fittin'." He smiled sheepishly. "I'll be glad to have you two attend and bolster up my nerve."

"I'll be right glad to stay," Stony said quickly. Tucson voiced similar words. . . .

By four-thirty that afternoon, Sam Dixon had been laid to his final rest. Tilford, in a dignified voice, had spoken the simple words that accompanied Sam Dixon to his last sleep, beside the other headstone beneath the spreading live oak. Quite a number of friends had arrived. In twos and threes they straggled back to the ranch house. Tilford stopped several men and with Tucson's consent, asked them to remain over for a time.

A while later, Tucson and Stony saddled up and started for Manzanita. Tilford came down to the corral with them. Tucson said, "Ringbone, you explain things to those who were asked to stay a spell. Now that your hands have returned with word that all the fellows you asked to attend our meeting will come, we should have quite a turnout. I'll be meeting them later."

"I sure hope everything goes off all right, Tucson," Tilford said dubiously. "One slip, and yo're done."

"Let me do the worrying on that score," Tucson smiled.

"If you was older, you might not be so confident." Tilford tried without success to match Tucson's smile. "At my age you realize what it means to buck a man like Matt Nirvan, and you never know when Lady Luck will turn a cold shoulder on you."

There was some further conversation, then Tucson and Stony lined their ponies out for

Manzanita. They sent their ponies into a swift lope. Now that the wheels had started to turn to get the plan rolling, Tucson didn't want to waste any more time. . . .

It was getting along toward ten o'clock that night when a cowpuncher entered the Golden Buck Saloon—the Golden Buck happening to be just one more of Matt Nirvan's ill-gained properties. There was quite a crowd in the barroom and the cowhand looked around for a few moments before he located Sheriff Beef Yarrow. Yarrow, at the moment, looked to be about three seas over from the liquor he'd taken aboard. The cowpuncher sidled up close to the sheriff and said in an undertone, "Matt wants you *pronto*, Beef."

Yarrow straightened with an effort and turned heavily around, shifting his cargo of hard liquor with difficulty. "Matt Nirvan wants me?" he hiccoughed.

"Shhh!" the cowhand whispered. "Not so loud. You trying to advertise it to the world?"

"Avertish wash t'worl'?" Yarrow blurted.

The cowpuncher drew Yarrow off to one side. "Here's the situation, Beef. Nirvan is making a strong play for public favor. He wants you to bring him a deputy's badge so he can do things legal."

"Dep'ty badge? Wha' for?" Owlishly, Yarrow eyed the man. "Who're you?" he inquired thickly.

"Never mind the name, Beef. I'm new on

Matt's payroll. Gunwork when needed, that's me. Now you'd better hurry or Matt will be sore as a boiled rooster. Matt wants you should bring him a deputy's badge. He's going to lay the murder of Dixon and Pete on Tucson Smith and his pals."

"Huuhn." Yarrow grunted skeptically, "Matt'll have to cash—catch—them hombres first."

"Catch 'em?" The other laughed scornfully. "Hell, Beef, he's already got 'em tied up tight in his office at the Purgatoire. And just in time too. Smith had a plan that would have raised merry hell with our set-up here—"

"T'hell you shay!" Yarrow's bloodshot eyes opened wider. "Matt captured all three of 'em? That's sure someshing!"

"You'll get the whole story later. But hurry up with that badge for Matt. He's going to pin it on, then parade Smith and his pals down to the jail. The word will go 'round that you appointed him a special deputy and that he made the catch singlehanded."

"Great idea, but—"

"Now, listen, it's all arranged. Once them three is in jail, some of us will be waiting out back of the building. It's fixed for Smith and his pards to escape. When they come running out, we'll cut 'em down with sawed-off shotguns—"

"What an idea!" Yarrow enthused.

"Ain't it! Matt sure uses his head. And it will be all legal. As a deputy, Nirvan will get a heap of praise that will reflect on you too. It will all be done in the course of duty—preventing a jail break. Now, hurry and get that badge. Matt's waiting to start."

"I'll have to go down to my offish—*hic!*—and get one. Maybe I'd better find Volpone too. He was here jush a few minutes ago."

"Volpone's at Matt's office, guardin' the prisoners and takin' healthy kicks at 'em while they're trussed up on the floor. You hurry and get that deputy badge. I'll slip back and let Matt know you're on your way."

Yarrow nodded and waddled toward the door of the Golden Buck, traces of excitement entering his small eyes. "I'll get the badge and a scattergun too," he promised himself. "I crave to pour some hot lead into that Smith hombre as much as the next man. And I won't be missshing no shots—*hic!*—at Smith's pals, neither."

XIV

Yarrow shoved his bulky form along the street as fast as his fat legs would carry him. Twice in the half gloom of the night street he bumped into pedestrians as he staggered along the walk. A few cowponies loped by, their riders jeering at the unsteady gait of the sheriff. Yarrow shook a thick fist at them and stumbled on his way.

His fleshy, unhealthy features worked spasmodically as he revolved in his muddled mind the various indignities he was going to inflict on one Tucson Smith, once he had him behind bars. By Gawd! He'd give him a damn' good beatin' first, before Tucson was shot. There wa'n't no uppity strange hombre goin' to come to Manzanita and monkey with Beef Yarrow.

And that Lullaby Joslin. Another fresh hombre. Thought he was right smart gettin' Pete killed that way and then walkin' right in to Matt's office to unload the body and hold up the whole bunch. Nirvan had been right riled about that. Yarrow cursed at thought of the things Nirvan had said about sheriffs who couldn't take care of their employers' interests better than allow a thing like that to happen.

"Dammit," Yarrow muttered thickly to himself, "how was I to know Joslin was going to pull a crazy trick like that? I was asleep. Matt should have informed me what was going on. Nope, he didn't have no right to curse me in such fashion, and b'Gawd I don't intend to take much more from him—"

Yarrow abruptly checked such thoughts and looked fearfully over one shoulder. Good Gawd! Supposin'—*hic!*—he'd actually faced up to Nirvan that way. There'd be hell to pay. A cold sweat burst on Yarrow's forehead. Dammit! It was all that Joslin's fault. Well, he'd get that Joslin too. And Stony Brooke. Them three cow nurses would be taught it don't pay to come into a town and start buckin' the big—*hic!*—boss.

Somethin' else them three would pay for too—the killin' of Corelli and Kraft. And half killin' poor Rabideau. They'd learn when their bodies was blown to hell with buckshot. It would be a lesson to other folks too who refused to buckle under to Matt. There was a heap of hombres who hated Matt these days. If all them fellers ever found a leader to organize 'em and started after Matt—Again a cold sweat burst on Yarrow's forehead.

He pulled out his bandanna and mopped at his wet face, commenced to rearrange his thoughts again. Well, Matt should be feelin' pretty good-natured about—*hic!*—now that he had them three captured. There'd be good money in hand for them that worked for Matt. Yarrow's spirits mounted once more. Screwing up his lips he started to whistle a tune he'd heard in a bawdy house.

By the time he'd reached his office he was feeling fine, humming away in an undertone that resembled to no small extent the buzzing of some savage hornet. Yessiree! Tucson Smith sure had a reckonin' due shortly. The door of Yarrow's office was unlocked. He stumbled inside and fumbled about for the lamp, then struck a match to the wick and replaced the chimney. That done he started to search through his desk for an odd deputy badge. Finally he found one, tucked away in an odd corner of a lower drawer. He rubbed it on his pant leg, hoping to remove some of the tarnish, but finally stuck it in a pocket and started to leave. Then he had another thought: Matt might like a pair of handcuffs to go with the badge. There were three pairs of handcuffs hanging on a nail. Now there was an idea. Matt like's not had those three hombres tied with rope. It would look more legal if handcuffs was used. Yarrow chuckled and distributed the handcuffs about his person. Then, blowing down the lamp chimney, he stepped from his doorway.

He was still humming cheerfully as he stepped outside and crossed the walk beneath the wooden awning overhead, intending to cut diagonally across the street. Then, just as he stepped to the roadway he heard, too late, the soft *swish* of a thrown rope, as a hempen loop settled about his shoulders, pinning his arms to sides as it tightened. A second rope dropped over his head. Yarrow opened his mouth to yell for help, but that second loop tightened about his throat, cutting off his breath. The cry ended in a thin, gasping squeak which resembled that of a frightened mouse. Two more hempen loops followed in quick succession and were drawn taut.

In no time at all, Sheriff Beef Yarrow was bound 'round like a trussed-up fowl.

Gasping for breath, Yarrow felt himself drawn up through the air. Dimly, through waning consciousness he heard someone say, "Don't pull by that rope 'round his neck. We want him alive." Low laughter followed.

A Mexican with unsteady steps, the result of one too many glasses of *tequila,* was the only pedestrian within hearing distance. The man's eyes bulged as he witnessed Yarrow swiftly whisked from the earth and jerked skyward to vanish in the gloom of night. Turning, he hurried for his small adobe home, and in the seclusion of this sanctuary, vowed never again to mix whiskey with his native *tequila.* Had he not witnessed the Señor Sheriff Yarrow taken off to Heaven? It was a visitation of the saints, no less! "Mark well, my Jovita," he spoke in a trembling voice to his wife, "with these two eyes I have seen an ascension. But why the *buen Dios* should take such as the

Señor Sheriff is beyond my understanding. But we shall never see him again. Never! It shall be a thing to relate to our grandchildren."

Meanwhile, four men on the roof of the sheriff's office tugged manfully to bring the struggling Yarrow to a flat surface. Despite their panting breaths, they could scarcely control their laughter. "Ease off on that throat rope, Lullaby," Tucson chuckled. "We don't want to strangle him."

"Oh, don't we?" came Lullaby's drawl.

"Not right off, anyway."

Lullaby slacked his grip on the rope. Yarrow took a deep, but still uneasy breath. He had sense enough not to try and cry for help a second time. Ten to one it was only some of the boys playing a joke on him. Maybe Volpone was back of this. Volpone had been acting right arrogant lately. Probably planning to get himself elected sheriff.

"Look out for his head, Stony," Tucson warned suddenly.

Bang! Yarrow's head struck one of the extending roof beams where it stuck out from the flat top of the adobe building. His body jerked sidewise, his hat falling off. His face scraped along the rough surface producing an abrasion. Yarrow groaned. His muddled mind had caught the single name, "Stony." That could mean but one thing. The cowboy who had come for the badge had lied! Matt Nirvan didn't have any prisoners. Yarrow's heart sunk. Now it was all up with him.

"Grab that off leg, Tucson," Stony was saying, "and we've got him. Gawd! What a weight! Bob, let go your rope and grab his gun."

There came a mighty heave and a tug and Beef Yarrow was hauled to the top and dragged to the flat roof surface. He started to sit up, but Tucson was on him like a flash, jamming a gun barrel in his middle. "Not a word out of you, Yarrow," Tucson threatened coldly. "One yell and it's your finish."

Yarrow's eyes rolled wildly but he made it plain he had no intention of yelling. "Did he bring the badge?" Lullaby wanted to know.

Tucson was going through Yarrow's pockets now. "Yeah, here it is." He slipped it into his own pocket. "Jeepers, we're in luck. He even brought three pairs of handcuffs."

"Fine," Stony laughed softly, "we'll find a use for 'em right now."

Yarrow was rolled on his face, arms behind him. A pair of cuffs were snapped on his wrists. A few minutes later he felt his boots being drawn off. Someone was trying to place handcuffs on his ankles too. Then Stony's panting voice, "Damn this hombre's fat hocks. I can't snap these bracelets. They're too tight."

"That's too bad," Tucson said unfeelingly.

"But what'll I do?"

"Snap 'em on," Lullaby suggested. "The flesh can be squeezed. Here, let me help you."

Yarrow groaned futilely as the cuffs were snapped shut. The four men sat down to rest a moment. The fourth one was known as Bob. Tucson drew a long breath. "Damned if that isn't more work than dipping beef animals."

"We should have had a derrick," Bob said.

"Pure hawg-fat," Stony put in.

Yarrow gurgled helplessly, turning his eyes toward the young cowboy known as Bob, and his heart came into his throat. It was the same fellow, all right, the one that had come to him in the Golden Buck with the fake message from Nirvan. Yarrow couldn't remember ever having seen him before.

Tucson guessed what was passing through Yarrow's mind. "Yep, he's a stranger, Beef. Just got a job on this range. We had to have somebody you didn't know, and Bob volunteered. You got suckered into something, Beef."

"You'll see, when I get free—" Yarrow commenced.

"I warned you to keep quiet, Beef," Tucson snapped. "Now you're really in for it."

"How true that is," from Stony. "No more easy money carrying out Nirvan's dirty schemes."

"Easy money?" Lullaby chuckled. "What more can Beef ask? He just got a raise, didn't he?"

“Raise, hell!” Stony countered. “That was a damned stiff haul.”

Tucson stood erect and glanced along the darkened street. There was no one in sight at the moment. “I think we’d better get started, fellows.”

“I’ll slip down and get things ready,” Bob volunteered. He went to the rear of the roof and slipped over the edge. Within a few more minutes, Yarrow had been lowered to the earth at the rear of his office. Five saddled horses waited there. It required but a minute longer to blindfold Yarrow and lay him across a saddle. There he was tied securely so he could not fall off.

“If you don’t know where you’re headed, Beef, so much the better,” Tucson told him. “Maybe you’re a mite uncomfortable, but you’ll live through it—for a little time, anyway.”

Yarrow nearly died from fear. This, he felt, was to be the end. Gawd! How could he get out of it? Tears filled his eyes, but he didn’t dare speak for fear Tucson would carry out the threat to shoot him. The horses got underway, heading down a back alley that ran parallel with the main street of Manzanita. Within a few minutes, Yarrow had lost all sense of direction. The jolting of the horse drove every thought from his head, save one—that he was shortly doomed to die.

XV

By the time Tucson and the others arrived back at the Wagon-Wheel, Yarrow was reduced to a quivering mass of jelly. He could scarcely stand when they lifted him down from the horse. A man on either side supported him. Yarrow heard low voices all around, but due to the blindfold couldn't see anyone. Men spoke bitterly of Nirvan's misdeeds and swore vengeance. Some of the voices sounded familiar, but Yarrow couldn't place them, and every time a mention of hanging or shooting was made, all memories were driven from Yarrow's craven soul.

Gradually, the voices grew silent. Footsteps retreated. The two men supporting Yarrow removed his handcuffs, after some search in the sheriff's pocket for the key, and told him to walk straight ahead. Yarrow was too frightened to try to escape, even if the thought had occurred to him. Now his one desire was to just remain alive, no matter where he was. He was led straight to the open doorway of the Wagon-Wheel barn which was eerily lighted with a number of candles. Then the door closed behind him. For a moment all was silence, but Yarrow had a feeling this place was filled with men, all thirsting for his life. His knees began to shake but he was prodded on.

After a moment he was stopped again and the blindfold was removed from his eyes. For a moment Yarrow could only blink his eyes as they became accustomed to the light. He knew now he was in a barn, but whose barn? Where was it? Uncertainly he looked around and his heart quickened beat as he saw a number of silent men, each wearing over his face a bandanna mask, through the eyeholes of which gleamed—in Yarrow's imagination—fiendish lights. With a shudder he averted his gaze from the sight, and then, on the door of the barn, Yarrow's bulging eyes saw a huge shadow—a shadow of hangman's noose.

Even as he looked on, horror-stricken, the looped shadow commenced a pendulum-like movement. From one side of the floor to the other it swayed. A shriek of terror left Yarrow's throat. In imagination he saw his own form suspended there, slowly swinging back and forth. He had no means of knowing that a cowhand up in the rafters had started the rope swinging. The terrified sheriff slumped to his knees and had to be lifted erect again.

He was half carried farther within the barn. The two who had escorted him, joined the group standing about the walls. Yarrow was left alone in the center of the floor. He glanced frantically about, like a cornered rat seeking some escape. Wherever he looked icy glances met his gaze.

No one spoke. There was now no movement save for the spiraling smoke of candles and the swinging back and forth of that terrible shadow. Yarrow was now standing directly in the path of the shadowy loop as it moved slowly from side to side. He could almost feel it tightening about his throat.

Yarrow summoned the few remnants of nerve he still possessed. He tried to hold the tones steady, indignant, but they quavered like an old man's when he spoke. "Wha—what does this mean?" he said weakly. "I'll—"

"Silence!" thundered a voice across the room.

Yarrow's knees knocked together. His teeth began to chatter. Cold beads of perspiration formed on his forehead.

Twelve men disengaged themselves from a group at the far wall, stepped out to confront Beef Yarrow. Raising his hands in fear, he began to back away. The twelve came to a stop a few yards away from the shaken Yarrow and stood staring at him, through their masks.

One of them advanced a step in front of the others. "Sheriff Yarrow," he spoke in deep sepulchral tones, "you are now standing in the presence of the Terrible Twelve. These other gentlemen stand ready to execute any order the Terrible Twelve may give them—even though such an order might mean your death."

"Wha—what for?" Yarrow gasped.

"That will be explained presently," the leader of the Twelve continued. Ringbone was speaking in the same impressive voice he had employed that afternoon in the reading of the service at Sam Dixon's burial, but to Yarrow the tones conveyed a far different meaning.

Tilford continued, "Yarrow, you have betrayed every trust reposed in you by the voters of Manzanita County. You are a disgrace to the badge you wear. The Terrible Twelve has been organized to combat the skulduggery of Matt Nirvan and his followers, and we find you guilty on several counts, ranging all the way from cheap thievery to accessory to murder. You have accepted money from Nirvan to conceal his crimes. What have you to say for yourself?"

"It ain't so, it ain't so," Yarrow cried brokenly. "It's all a mistake. I wouldn't do nothin' like that."

"Each word I have spoken is truth!" Tilford thundered. "Within a short time, Matt Nirvan and his followers will be standing in the spot you now occupy so cravenly. We are giving a fair trial and passing judgment on each of you. Have you anything to say regarding why sentence should not be passed on you immediately?"

Yarrow sank to his knees, clasped hands raised in terror. "For Gawd's sake, give me a chance. I'll do anything you say. I—"

Tilford cut brusquely in, turning to the room

at large. “Gentlemen of the Twelve, and others, what sentence do you pass on this man you see before you?”

“Death! Death by the rope!” The words boomed forth in one mighty voice, shaking the rafters of the building. “Death!”

Beef Yarrow swayed, then slumped to the floor, mouth open in fear. He moaned and then lay silent.

Tucson turned to Stony. “Cripes! The scut fainted. I reckon Tilford won’t have to go through with all that rigamarole that we planned.”

A cowhand hurried to get a pail of water. Tilford approached Tucson, removing his mask and wiping with a bandanna the perspiration beneath. “The bluff is working better than I thought it would, Tucson,” he smiled grimly. “I reckon by the time they bring Yarrow out of that faint, he’ll be ready to cooperate. He’s sure scared.”

“Scared plenty,” Tucson nodded.

The cowhand returned with the bucket of water and dashed it over the unconscious Yarrow. Yarrow rolled on his face, then, sputtering, managed to scramble upright. Tilford hurried across the floor to once more confront him.

For a moment Yarrow’s mind swam, and he couldn’t remember where he was, then as his wet gaze once more focused on the figures of the Terrible Twelve, he fell to his knees, pleading for clemency. His lips drooled and he howled like an injured cur. Several of the cowmen turned away in disgust. Tilford spoke quick orders. Two men lifted the terrified Yarrow to his feet, holding him erect.

"Yarrow, you have just one chance for your life," Tilford stated in stern tones.

Lights of hope came to Yarrow's eyes. His cries for mercy changed to a debased whimpering. "I'll do anything—anything you Twelve men say," he sobbed brokenly.

"Yarrow," Tilford continued coldly, "you were legally placed in office, but the time has come for you to leave the country. To displace you would require a great deal of red tape. If we asked you to resign, any promise you'd make would be useless. But you've got to go away, as far from Manzanita as possible."

"I'll do it, Mr. Twelve, I'll do it," Yarrow cried.

Tilford smiled beneath his mask. "I'm going to dictate a couple of papers you'll have to sign. Sign them, and we'll release you. Otherwise—" Without finishing the words, Tilford solemnly indicated the slowly swinging shadow of the hempen loop.

"I'll sign 'em, I'll sign 'em," Yarrow promised frantically.

A large packing case to serve as a desk was carried before Yarrow. Lullaby, face masked, seated himself with pen, paper and a bottle of ink. Tilford turned to the ashen-faced Yarrow. "To elect a new sheriff now would entail an unnecessary expense and take some time. Yarrow, you're leaving, but we demand that you appoint Tucson Smith a deputy of Manzanita County, with full power to make arrests and to enforce the law in any manner he sees fit. Are you willing to do it?"

"I'll do it, Mister Twelve."

Tucson, unmasked, approached the desk and stood close to Yarrow, the sheriff unwilling to meet his eyes. Tilford ordered, "Sheriff Yarrow, administer the oath of office."

Tucson raised his right hand. Yarrow commenced in a trembling voice, "Tucson Smith, do you solemnly swear and promise to uphold the laws—" Here Yarrow gulped and struggled for words. His voice fell lower and lower, but somehow he managed to limp through the oath to the end. Tucson lowered his hand. The deputy's badge of office was pinned to his vest.

Next, Tilford turned to Lullaby and commenced to dictate: "I, B.F. Yarrow, duly and legally elected sheriff of Manzanita County, do hereby state and declare that I have appointed Tucson Smith a deputy of said county to have full authority to act in any way he sees fit in enforcing the law. Deputy Tucson Smith's authority is to have precedence over the authority of any other deputy in the county." Tilford paused, "I reckon that disposes of anything Trent Volpone might try."

He continued dictating. "This statement is signed of my own free will and accord, and in the frank opinion that Deputy Smith will fill this office, in my absence, more ably than I could myself. In signing this statement I wish to say it is necessary to vacate my office for a time due to reasons of health, and that I have not been forced, or in any way coerced"—here a snicker escaped Lullaby, busy with the pen—"in any manner whatever, to act thusly in this matter, but am doing it with the thought that the greatest good for all may be served. Signed, B.F. Yarrow."

Tilford whispered to Tucson, "Does that sound legal enough?"

"It's fine. It's the kind of fire we need to fight fire."

Tilford swung back to Yarrow. "Sign it, Beef." He added to Lullaby, "Write 'Signed in the presence of the following witnesses,' across from Yarrow's signature."

Yarrow picked up the pen with trembling fingers, hesitated.

Tucson said, "You know, Yarrow, you don't have to sign if you don't want to. You have to do it of your own free will."

At that moment, the cowboy up in the rafters started the hempen loop swinging even more violently, the grisly shadow sweeping ominously across the desk. Yarrow gave a sudden frightened start. "I'll sign, I'll sign," he quavered.

Gripping the pen in a hand that shook, he affixed in wobbly writing, *"B.F. Yarrow, Sheriff of Manzanita County."*

Twelve men, including Tilford, signed as witnesses.

"There's one more paper you'll have to write yourself, Yarrow. Sit down at the desk."

Yarrow seated himself. Lullaby supplied fresh paper and pen.

Tilford said, "You'll have to write a note to Nirvan, Yarrow." He dictated, "Dear Matt—Owing to the sudden death of my beloved Aunt Minnie, I've got to go away for a spell. My deputy will have full charge of everything in my absence. Yours truly, Beef Yarrow."

Yarrow wrote and signed the letter. Finished, he said dumbly, "But I ain't got no Aunt Minnie, Mister Twelve."

The room erupted in uncontrolled laughter. Yarrow was beginning to recover his composure. Tucson said, "Don't worry about the Aunt Minnie part, Yarrow. Nirvan won't know the difference, because I don't figure you'll see him for a long time—if ever. If you ever return to this part of the country, we'll carry out the judgment voted on you tonight That's fair warning."

Tilford added, "You're due for a long ride, Yarrow, and we want that you should get ridin' right off. Don't ever stop ridin' until yo're sure in yore mind you ain't never comin' back. That clear?"

Yarrow nodded and they escorted him out to the corral where he was placed on a horse. Tucson struck the animal across the rump and the beast started. And ride Yarrow did. Once free, he urged the pony to even greater efforts—taking a direction entirely opposite to that which led towards Manzanita.

Masks discarded, a large number of men stood listening to the staccato pounding of pony's hoofs which grew fainter and ever fainter until they'd disappeared completely.

"He won't ever come back," Tilford said grimly. "He's scared spitless. Your bluff worked fine, Tucson."

Tucson nodded. "With the help of the set-up you arranged. I figured it would. I had a hunch Yarrow was a weak link in the Nirvan chain of crooks. Ringbone, you certainly acted your part swell. The old hokum worked great."

"Yeah, it worked," Tilford admitted sheepishly, "but I shore felt like an idiot handin' out that *habla* about the Terrible Twelve foolishness."

"Didn't I say it was hokum?" Tucson chuckled. "Yarrow was just the type to be awed by that sort of a performance."

Tilford looked serious. "I wonder if that paper he signed would stand up in court?"

"Probably not," Tucson said promptly, "but

who's going to take it to court? Nirvan? He wouldn't dare. I'd sure relish to see him take it to court."

"I reckon you're right," Tilford agreed. "Too bad Rawlins, of the Rocking-R, was sick and couldn't be on hand. But sending his brother, Bob, to help out, was fine. It made a good introduction to a new country for Bob."

Lullaby said, "That paper Yarrow signed should be put in a safe spot, but how about having a copy made that could be stuck on the courthouse door where everybody could see it?"

"That's a right idea, Lullaby," Tucson nodded, "but let's hold off a day or so. I want to announce to Volpone he has a new deputy over him first. We'll let the Nirvan gang learn the news as we go along. But that note to Nirvan should be sent in soon."

"I'll take it in," Lullaby offered.

"No you don't," Stony protested. "Look what happened the last time we left you alone in town. You got Pete killed and then made a damn' fool of yourself acting arrogant in Nirvan's office. You might have got hurt yourself. Only that you had the devil's own luck—oh, cripes! you're just too stupid to realize when you're in danger."

The others laughed, gathering around. All appeared cheerful now that it looked as though Nirvan would have someone to buck him. Most of them shook hands and wished Tucson luck in his new deputy job. Tucson thanked them. “I’m counting on all of you,” he said. “We’re not out of the woods yet, and I’m going to need plenty help. But, now, at least, we’ve got a legal stand in our fight against the Nirvan outfit—and there’s nothing I’d sooner do than throw legal lead in the right direction.”

XVI

Noon of the following day found only a scattering of customers drinking at the bar in the Purgatoire. Matt Nirvan stood by himself at one end, answering only in monosyllables when the bartender or anyone else spoke to him. He nursed a glass of whiskey in moody silence, his pasty features drawn with lines of thought. Trent Volpone came hurrying in and joined him at the bar. Nirvan looked up, but dropped his head again, without speaking.

"Damned if I can find Beef," Volpone grumbled. "Looked all over for the fat buzzard. The bartender at the Golden Buck said he was in there last night, until some cowpunch come in and talked to him a few minutes. Then Beef left like he had urgent business. The bartender says he heard your name mentioned once, and he figures you had sent for Beef."

"Who was the cowpunch?" Nirvan asked.

Volpone shook his head. "Stranger. The bartender had never seen him before."

"Too damn many strangers coming in lately," Nirvan growled.

"Where do you suppose Beef's gone to?"

"Maybe attendin' his Aunt Minnie's funeral by this time."

"Huh? What you talking about, Matt?"

"I've had word from Beef," Nirvan said in ugly tones. He handed Volpone a folded note. "This had been shoved under the door when we opened up this morning. Haven't any idea who brought it. Maybe Beef himself left it before he took off—"

"Took off—?"

"Read the note, dammit!"

Volpone unfolded the paper, eyes scanning the writing. "What in hell—" he muttered. The note read:

> *Dear Matt—Owing to the sudden death of my beloved Aunt Minnie, I got to go away for a spell. My deputy will have full charge of everything in my absence. Yours truly, Beef Yarrow.*

Volpone stared at Nirvan and handed back the note. Nirvan tore it into small pieces and flung them on the floor.

Volpone said in a puzzled tone, "That's damn funny—"

"That all you can say, Trent?" Nirvan scowled. "I don't see anything funny about it."

"What I mean is, Beef always told me he didn't have any relatives. Could be he was so fat, there wasn't enough left over for any more in the family." Volpone essayed a weak laugh.

"God, you're funny," Nirvan said bitterly.

"What I want to make sure of, is that note really in Beef's handwriting?"

"Oh, it was Beef's writing all right. I recognized some of those fancy hooks he puts on his writing. No doubt—"

Nirvan's clenched fist landed on the bar. Men drinking farther along the counter looked around. Nirvan lowered his voice: "That settles it then. Aunt Minnie my ashcan! Beef just got yellow and sloped off. Just because we haven't had good breaks lately, he lost his nerve. He was getting skeery of Smith and the other two. The things they pulled threw a bad jolt into Beef."

"Yes, I reckon. I could see him slippin'. What do we do now?"

"I've been thinking about it. After all is said and done, I've concluded that we're better off without Beef—especially now that he's gone yellow. His note said you'd have charge of everything. We'll leave it that way. You'll handle his job. Go 'long obeying orders like you've always done. When election comes up I'll see that you get elected sheriff of the county."

"Suits me, Matt. I've always felt Yarrow was a weak sister. Fat, slow and lazy. And lacked guts. Now you've got a crew you can depend on, one hundred percent."

"We'll be better off," Nirvan nodded. "I won't have Beef bellyaching every time I want something arranged. He was always afraid that some county official might find out how things were going here. I'm glad he left. T'tell the truth, before you verified his handwriting, I was a mite afraid that Smith and his pards might have kidnaped him and forged that note."

"Not a chance. We've got to give Smith credit for that much brains. Getting rid of Beef would just put me in charge." He paused, then, "What's the next move, Matt?"

"I can tell better when Smith and his pards show up. I've had a couple of men out spying, but they haven't uncovered them. Don't know where they are. By the way, Trent, do you know anybody named Rawlins—a cowhand?"

"Sure, Rawlins who runs the Rocking-R."

Nirvan shook his head. "No. This is a Bob Rawlins. I saw him coming out of Ortega's General Store this morning, right after I'd opened up. Had an idea maybe he'd left that note. I crossed over and asked Ortega who he was. Ortega had never seen him before. Said Rawlins had just come in for a sack of goober nuts, paid for 'em and left."

"Probably some saddle-tramp riding through."

Nirvan agreed and after talking a few minutes longer, Volpone headed for the sheriff's office.

An hour later, Tucson, accompanied by Lullaby and Stony, rode into Manzanita. The two dropped off at the Brown Bottle and Tucson continued on to the sheriff's office.

Arriving there, Tucson stopped a moment to gaze at the plaque at the side of the doorway, which gave Yarrow's name as sheriff and Volpone's as deputy. At that moment the sound of snoring struck Tucson's ears. Peering through the open doorway he saw Trent Volpone stretched out in the sheriff's chair, spurred boots propped on the desk. Volpone's eyes were closed. His mouth opened and shut at regular intervals as the snores issued forth.

Tucson leaned against the doorjamb considering the scene, chuckling. "Sounds for all the world like a slow freight climbing a steep grade. That little whistling sound Volpone ends up with every time makes it plumb realistic."

His attention went back to the small sign near the doorway: B.F. Yarrow, Sheriff—Trent Volpone, Deputy-Sheriff. Tucson considered a moment, then taking a stub of lead-pencil from his pocket, he drew several heavy lines through the names of the two men. Near the words, Deputy-Sheriff, he carefully printed his own name.

"That takes care of that," he smiled and entered the office. Volpone continued his snoring. Tucson gave the room a quick survey, nose wrinkling with disgust. Everything was covered with dust. The floor was littered with cigar and cigarette stubs, burnt matches, bits of yellowed paper. The reward bills tacked on the wall were fly-specked and faded. A topographical map of the county, at the back wall, was torn, one loose section hanging nearly to the floor. Two cots were ranged along the side and back walls. The blankets were rumpled and hadn't been shaken out or folded in months.

"A *muy elegante* hawg-wallow," was Tucson's disdainful verdict.

He glanced about for a broom. There wasn't any. He left the building, went to the general store and purchased one. Then he returned. Volpone was still asleep; he didn't look as though he'd moved since Tucson first saw him.

Then Tucson set to work. The dust gathered, rolled up in clouds. He removed his sombrero, rolled up his sleeves and attacked the dirt with renewed energy. Tobacco butts, old papers, match stubs and dust went flying through the open doorway. Dust motes swirled violently in the office.

Still Volpone didn't awaken. He smelled of liquor. Perhaps that had something to do with it. Finally, the dust penetrated his nostrils. He coughed, choked and began a furious sneezing. Finally he removed his boots from the desk and sat up, cursing and blinking his eyes. He didn't for the moment see Tucson, then hearing the sounds of the broom he started to glance around.

"Howdy, Volpone," Tucson said cheerfully. "I

was beginning to think you were dead. It didn't smell too good in here. Right good thing you came alive. I was just on the point of sweeping you out."

The chair turned over with a crash as Volpone bounded to his feet. "What in hell do you think you're doing?" he demanded.

"There's been a dirty law administration that needs a cleaning out," Tucson explained gravely, pausing to rest on the end of the broom handle. "I've just gone into politics, Volpone, and it's amazing how much dirt a man can uncover when he digs into things. Now, just stand to one side please, while I get this broom under the desk." *Swish, swish, swish* went the broom. A cloud of dust billowed from the floor.

Volpone eyed Tucson in bewilderment and growing anger. Suddenly he exclaimed, "Hey! Cut that out!"

Tucson halted in pretended surprise. "You maintaining you like to be dirty?"

"What I like is my business," Volpone retorted hotly.

"Dirty business, hombre, dirty business," Tucson said reprovingly. He put down the broom, pointed to the badge on his open vest. "After all the trouble I took to shine it up, too," he complained in hurt tones, "you haven't even noticed it."

Volpone's jaw dropped, his eyes bugged out.

"Where did—did you g-g-get that?" he stammered. "What's it mean?"

"Don't tell me you can't recognize a deputy badge—"

"You know damn' well I do," Volpone said furiously, "but—"

"It means that I'm a duly appointed deputy-sheriff of Manzanita County."

"Who appointed you?" Volpone snapped.

"Who else but the sheriff of the county?"

"Beef Yarrow?"

"None other."

"Damn it, I can't believe that."

"Well, you see, Volpone, Beef had to leave sudden-like, owing to the death of his beloved Aunt Minnie—"

"By God, now I know you had something to do with that—"

"With Aunt Minnie's death?" Tucson's eyebrows lifted. "Why I've never even seen the dear old soul—"

"You—you—you"—Volpone's anger mounted—"you know what I mean—Beef leaving sudden the way he did. I'll bet you forced him to write that note."

"Oh, my, no," Tucson said sadly. "You don't know how bad I felt when Yarrow announced he was about to depart this vale of sin and iniquity."

"You're a liar!"

Tucson refused to get nettled. "Yeah, I am," he

admitted cheerfully. “I could have let out yelps of joy when Yarrow lit out. The fact remains, he appointed me his deputy—and to take precedence over you—”

“I don’t believe it.”

Tucson sighed. “Seeing is believing.” He took from his pocket a folded paper. “Read that.”

Volpone’s scowl increased as he read the written words. Angry color flooded his temples. He went white, then red again. “Hell,” he sneered, “this ain’t worth the paper it’s written on. That’s not Beef’s writing.” Defiantly, he ripped the paper to shreds and hurled them to the floor.”

“Tch! tch!” Tucson reproved. “Now you’ve made more work for me. Of course, that’s not Beef’s writing. That’s just a copy. The original is where it can be produced when needed. There’ll be another copy posted at the courthouse in a day or so. Now get out of the way, while I finish redding up this pigpen—”

“By Gawd, I just can’t believe it.” Some of the wind had been taken from Volpone’s sails with the reading of the paper. “I’d have to work under you?”

“That’s what Beef said.”

“I refuse to work under such conditions—”

“You never *worked* under *any* conditions,” Tucson said contemptuously, and picked up his broom again.

“I’m quitting right now.”

"Had an idea you would. That's why I removed your name from the sign."

The words maddened Volpone. He dashed to the doorway, took one look at the plaque beside the entrance. His features went purple. He whirled back into the office where Tucson was nonchalantly sweeping. He started to reach for his gun, but thought better of it. Now nothing would satisfy him but to get his clenched fingers about Tucson's throat.

Swinging his arms he rushed, like an enraged bull, at Tucson. Tucson laughed and quickly sidestepped. As Volpone passed, carried by his impetus, Tucson stuck the handle of the broom between the enraged man's legs.

Tripping, Volpone went crashing down with a thud that shook the building. Tucson stepped to one side, stood his broom in one corner and calmly waited for Volpone to get to his feet. He rose slowly, shaking his head, then with a sudden mad rush, closed in, fists swinging.

Again, Tucson sidestepped easily, his right fist shot out, catching Volpone on the side of the head and bounced him against the doorjamb. Tucson swung his left, whirled Volpone around, and gave him the right again.

That final blow turned the trick. Volpone went staggering backward through the open doorway, legs working furiously to regain his balance—back, back, across the office porch and sidewalk, until with a thud the man's back struck the crossbar of the hitchrail. But his impetus was too great to be stopped. For just a brief moment his body paused, then both legs rose in the air and, heels over head, Trent Volpone landed with a crash in the roadway.

For a moment he lay stunned. Blood trickled from his face and bruised lips. Tucson came outside, moved around the end of the hitchrail, stooped down and ripped the deputy's badge from Volpone's shirt.

"Want some more, Volpone?" he demanded. "If so, get up and take it. I'm not asking for your resignation. I'm firing you!"

Bracing himself on elbows, Volpone glowered up at Tucson, as he came to a sitting position. Abruptly, his right hand reached to his gunbutt. But Tucson had foreseen that maneuver. His booted foot shot out, pinning Volpone's wrist to the earth. Volpone uttered an agonized yelp, released hold on his gun and fell back.

"I could have killed you for that move, Volpone," Tucson said grimly, "but we'll let it pass right now. Get out of here!"

There'd been wild yells along the street a moment after Volpone struck the roadway. A small crowd began to collect. Bloodshot eyes glaring madly, Volpone slowly got to his feet and backed away, holding his bruised wrist with his left hand. "I've had enough," he conceded, adding under his breath, "right now."

"Let me know when you're ready for more," Tucson laughed shortly. His gaze followed Volpone as the man lurched off down the street, barging roughly into people. Bystanders on both sides of the street stopped to look. A latecomer came hurrying up. "Trouble 'round here?" he wanted to know. "Volpone looked like he was on the prod."

"Did act sort of put out, didn't he?" Tucson smiled.

"Sure did. Ain't you afraid he'll arrest you, mister?"

Tucson shook his head. "I just removed his authority. I'm running things in Sheriff Yarrow's place for a spell. Beef has suffered a bereavement and won't be around for a time, so he appointed me to handle things. I've just been cleaning up a mite. Reckon I'll go finish up, now."

The crowd drifted away as Tucson retreated to the office and closed the door. For an hour or more he labored. He mopped the office and set the room to rights, then seated himself at the desk and went through papers that should have been put in order long since. By the time he'd finished he had some inkling of what his new job entailed. Then he stepped out to the street, locking the door behind him and placing a key in his pocket.

Pausing a moment to roll and light a cigarette he considered his next move. "I guess I'd better drift down and tell Nirvan that Manzanita has a new law officer. Volpone has already told him, but I'll make it official." He drew three cheerful puffs on the cigarette, then ground the butt under his boot toe. That done, he strode purposefully down the street to the Purgatoire.

XVII

It was well after three in the afternoon when Tucson drew abreast of the big honkytonk. A few loiterers eyed him curiously as he boldly ascended the short flight of steps to the double-doored entrance. Just within the doorway he paused a moment, his gaze taking in the interior. It was too early in the day for much business. The gaming tables and wheels were encased in oilcloth coverings. The orchestra stand was deserted. At one side, one of the dance hall girls sat on a table, filing her fingernails. She'd not yet donned her short-skirted costume of the evening, and at present was dressed in modest gingham. She was carrying on a desultory conversation with Bronc Rabideau and Trent Volpone, who sat on straight-backed chairs on either side of the table. Volpone's face was bruised and he had a bandanna wrapped around his right wrist. Rabideau's left arm was in a sling. A padded look under the new denims on his left thigh indicated a bandage. Rabideau looked rather pale but also appeared capable of getting about, if necessary. Tucson concluded the man could still prove dangerous.

Lined along the bar were Black Payette, Riker Wetzel, Santone, Shive Otis and Matt Nirvan. All had their backs turned and were concentrating on the glasses before them. A bartender silently mopped the bar and prepared to put out another bottle if called for. A few other customers were scattered along the bar nearer the front.

For a moment, no one noticed Tucson. Then the girl gave a short startled squeak that aroused the others. "It gave me a start seeing him there, watching us," she explained, coloring. As one man the others had turned. Rabideau and Volpone got to their feet then sat down again.

Nirvan scowled. "What do you want, Smith?"

"Talk," Tucson said briefly. "I'll do the talking and you listen."

"You starting trouble?"

"*You* started it. I'm aiming to finish it."

"That's for you to say. And I suppose your pards are outside waiting to jump in, in case we don't like what you say."

"You're free to think anything you want."

"Could I get what I want by thinking," Nirvan sneered, "you wouldn't be here." He was puzzled. Tucson didn't appear to be starting anything. What was his object in coming to the Purgatoire? Then, Nirvan smiled. Every man had his price. So that was it. He went on, "I understand you're the law here now."

"You understand correct."

Nirvan said bluntly, "What's your price?"

"For what?"

"For minding your own business."

"That I do for nothing, Nirvan, and my business at present it to see that Manzanita gets a law-abiding existence."

Nirvan gave a short scornful laugh. "Sure, that talk's fine for the town's ears, but you can speak out. Pretend you're among friends. Look at it this way. I've got plenty of cash and I intend to have more. Somebody's got to run this town. I'm already in the saddle and I figure to stay there. So what's your price for leaving me alone?"

"For leaving you alone?" Tucson smiled. "My price is that you take your pack of coyotes and clear out of Manzanita. Decent folks don't want you here. If you're smart, you'll leave now, before something happens that prevents you from leaving—except feet first."

An angry growl ran through the room. Tucson waited, acting as though he'd not heard it. Nirvan snapped, "You're just crazy as a *locoed* steer, Smith. You can't set up to run me out."

"I've got the authority to do just that. So you'd best wind up your affairs and get out soon's possible. I've fired Volpone and made that stick. Why not? Yarrow appointed me, all legal. You can't beat that."

Nirvan laughed sarcastically. "Yeah, Trent told me about that. But I'm not worried. Yarrow is gone, and without him to prove it, your word isn't worth a damn."

"We've got Yarrow's witnessed statement. I brought in a copy to show, but Volpone tore it up. Maybe he told you about it. We're having another copy made to post at the courthouse."

"Copies! copies!" Nirvan sneered. "They don't prove a thing. How do I know you didn't make up the whole business? I'll take you into court and make you produce the original."

Tucson smiled thinly. "That's just fine, Nirvan. Bring on your court. The sooner the better. And how do you think you'll show up in a court of law when the truth about conditions here is given air?"

Nirvan's face went red, then white, then crimsoned again. He started to speak. Opened his mouth and shut it. And again. Until he began to take on the effect of a gasping fish out of water.

The girl on the table tittered. "That's known as calling a bluff," she laughed. "Mister Smith, how about you and me getting better acquainted? You'll lose out in the long run, but I sure admire your spunk."

"Thanks, sister," Tucson chuckled. "It's the regret of my life that I can't take you up on your offer, but I'm too busy right now. Later, perhaps."

"That's a nice line of blarney too," the girl dimpled, "but I'd like to hear more—"

"Shut your trap!" Nirvan glared at the girl. "Somebody throttle that skirt."

Rabideau spoke quickly to the girl and she

shrank back, all laughter gone from her eyes. Tucson spoke scornfully, "Now you're in your own class, Nirvan—bullying women."

"By God, Smith, I don't have to take that—"

"You'll take it and like it. I said I was going to do the talking. Now you listen! You *know* I've got the authority to close you up, but I'd just as soon you'd stay and get what's coming to you. The Purgatoire is a blot on Manzanita. From now on you'll close at midnight prompt. I've been hearing things about the way you treat your girls. That's got to stop! Your games have got to be run honestly. I'm warning you now that this war is full-fledged and you're losing the battle, just as sure as Mr. Sam Colt made little lead pills to cure diseases like you. Sure, I admit it. I'm out to get you! Why aren't you man enough to fight your own battles, instead of hiring your killers. Don't you know how to use a gun? Are you yellow—?"

"No, by Jesus!" Nirvan exploded. "I'm not afraid to do anything my men do, but it's my motto to never do anything myself I can hire done. I know more about fanning gun smoke than you ever did, and if the time ever comes for you to face me, man to man—"

"You sure do toss a healthy boast," Tucson cut in, "but we'll beat you and your hired help as well. We've licked you at every turn of the cards. Your ambushing scheme fell through. You set two knifemen to fire the Brown Bottle. Lullaby

Joslin made a fool of you that time. He came here and made monkeys of the lot of you. Nirvan, you'd better face the fact you're beaten. We're fast organizing men, men who are determined to stand for you and your ways no longer. That's my warning. You'd better take it. That's all!"

While Tucson had been talking, Volpone's anger had grown until it seemed ready to explode within his skull. Throwing caution to the winds, he came erect, reaching for his gun, just as Tucson was turning away from Nirvan.

Tucson caught the girl's half-choked warning cry, as Rabideau slapped one hand across her mouth.

"Don't try it, Volpone!" Tucson snapped.

But Volpone was beyond hearing, his gun already half out of holster. Tucson's right hand flashed down, up. He felt the weapon kick in his hand. Once! Twice!

Even as Volpone pulled trigger, the solid impact of Tucson's leaden slugs flung him half around, causing his shot to whine wildly across the bar, shattering a pyramid of drinking glasses on the back bar and bringing a frantic scattering of the men who'd been standing near Nirvan and Tucson but a moment before. Nirvan himself dropped flat, as did Santone. The others scampered for their lives.

Volpone plunged down, landing on one shoulder, then rolled over and lay still. Black powder smoke swirled through the room. The girl screamed. Somebody cursed.

By the time the others had gained their wits, Tucson had backed toward the doorway, his gun covering the lot. Nirvan scrambled up from the floor, face pasty white, arms in air. The others followed suit. Tucson said, "Volpone asked for it. Are you going to be fool enough to do the same?" No one answered. Tucson went on. "I don't reckon a doctor could do Volpone any good now. Either way, take care of him, Nirvan. He's been your man right along. See it through. That's an order."

The others stood speechless as he backed to the front wall, then sidled along until he had reached the open doorway, still facing them, leveled Colt gun in hand.

Then, in a flash he was gone and out on the street. Wetzel and Payette started for the door, but Nirvan called them back. Santone glanced at them, something of contempt in his eyes. He crossed to the still form of Trent Volpone and stooped down.

After a minute he rose. "Trent's finished, Matt," he said tonelessly, "and you'd better do some fast thinking or we'll all be riding in the same hearse."

XVIII

Trent Volpone's body was carried away by a couple of loiterers Nirvan beckoned in from the street. With that done, Nirvan went to the bar and downed two fast slugs of whiskey. After a time he began to breathe easier. Only men of his own hiring were left in the barroom now. The girl had vanished up the flight of stairs that mounted to the second floor at one wall. The others waited for Nirvan to speak.

Cold fury possessed him as he started to speak. "A fine crew I've got," he snapped caustically. "Yellow, every one of you. What way is that to back me? Letting Smith get away when we had him right inside the Purgatoire. Volpone was the only one that had the nerve to—"

"Yeah"—Santone didn't appear greatly impressed by the tirade—"and look what happened to Volpone. Sure, we played safe—as any smart man would do. That shot of Volpone's might have hit any one of us, flying wild like it did. That was a numbskull trick. He didn't stop to think. He just went crazy mad for a minute. Volpone was a fool. He wouldn't have tried anything either, even then, except he thought Smith was off-guard—"

"If that fool woman hadn't yelped—" Nirvan began.

“The girl had nothing to do with it. I was watching Smith. There wasn’t an instant he didn’t know what was going on, all around. You can say what you like, Matt, but I’m admitting Smith is fox-smart, and I got a sneaking admiration for him.”

Nirvan swore an oath. “That’s just the trouble,” Nirvan rasped. “You call it admiring him. I figure he’s got you buffaloed.”

Santone uttered a short scornful laugh. “I didn’t see you starting anything, Matt—and what Smith told you was plenty frank and to the point.”

Nirvan’s pasty face colored. “I’m paying you hombres to do the fighting. Hell! Did you think I was handing you all charity?” The others didn’t speak. Nirvan continued, with a long sigh. “Yep, I reckon it was charity, as nobody’s earning his pay. I’m beginning to think you’re all yellow.”

“That’s enough, Matt!” Santone’s voice cracked like a whiplash.

Nirvan subsided then said, sullenly, “Well?”

“Listen, Matt, I’ve got eleven notches cut in my gunbutt.”

“Well?” Nirvan waited.

“I didn’t cut those notches for reminders of times I’ve attended sewing bees.”

“Well?”

“Yeah—it is well,” Santone said placidly. “Those notches represent some of the best gun-fighters in the country—San Antonio, Tombstone, Tascosa, Las Vegas, Abilene, Dodge City, Laredo, El Paso, Cripple Creek—"

"You sound like a train announcer," Nirvan sneered. "I don't remember asking for any geography lesson. So you've been around. What happened to you up in Cheyenne—?"

"Two was more than I could handle," Santone admitted cheerfully. "After I recovered I came down here. Knowing what I do now I'd have been better off to have kept going."

"Now, Santone, don't get proddy. What you heading at?"

"I'm making it clear that I've dropped some of the fastest men in the cow country. You know I'm the fastest gun in your stable. Why not let me go after Smith? You've played around with a lot of cockeyed schemes that have all gone haywire. The thing to do is forget those fancy plans, and go after Smith in straightforward fashion. Once Smith is out of the way I can start whittling down his two pards—"

"Think you can do it?" Nirvan was becoming interested.

"You know my record," Santone said quietly. "I figure Smith might be pretty good—he drew fast on Volpone. But I can draw faster. Let me go to Smith and challenge him to shoot it out. A clean break for both sides and none of your underhanded stunts. Could be you can't understand anything that old-fashioned, but I was raised in the old-fashioned school of gun-fighting."

"Maybe you're right," Nirvan said thoughtfully. He glanced at the others. "What do you boys think?" They nodded. One of them said something in praise of Santone's speed. Nirvan's obsidian eyes narrowed. "We could try it. And just in case you slip up, we could have a good man with a Winchester hid to finish off your job."

Santone swore. His temper rose. "Damn it, no, Matt. That's what I don't like about your methods. I'm no angel, I've lived by my gun, but I never lived snake-sneaky. You let me handle this."

"What's your plan?"

"Nothing involved about it. I'll slip along to the Brown Bottle, or wherever I can find Smith, and plain-out tell him this town isn't big enough to hold both of us. I'll give him one hour to pull out or take the consequences. If he wants to stay, we can shoot it out on Main Street. With a plan like that I can't help beating Smith to the draw. He's outfoxed us so far, but no man can outfox a lead slug."

Nirvan shrugged. "It's worth trying I guess. Go ahead. Make your war talk to Smith."

Santone nodded, turned away, mounted the stairs to his room on the second floor. When he returned he had a second six-shooter stuck in the waistband of his trousers. Nirvan looked queerly at him. "Looks like you're really prepared for war, Santone."

"Something like that," Santone said shortly. He wheeled toward the door. "I'll be seeing you shortly."

The instant he was out of sight, Nirvan turned to Wetzel. "Riker, you go find old Hugo Riley. There's no better rifleshot in town than old Hugo. Have him bring his smoke-pole and hide in that empty 'dobe shack between here and the Brown Bottle. If Smith should have the luck to drop Santone, Riley can drop Smith. Make it clear I'll pay a bonus over the usual."

Wetzel hesitated. "That's just the kind of thing that Santone was objectin' to, Matt. I figure—"

"Damn it, are you working for me or for Santone? I'll do the figuring that's done on this outfit. Santone is all right when it comes to fanning a gun, but he can't plan worth a damn. I want to make this thing sure, see? Now you go find Riley and hurry up about it. We don't need to let Santone know. By God, Riker, you'll do as I say or I'll—"

Wetzel shrank from Nirvan's wrath. "Right, chief. You're the boss."

Tucson had scarcely left the Purgatoire, after downing Trent Volpone, when he saw Lullaby and Stony running toward him, their faces torn with anxiety. By this time quite a number of people were heading toward the Purgatoire. Excited yells were heard along the street. The instant they spied Tucson, the two slowed down. Tucson hastened to meet them.

"What's up?" Stony asked. Lullaby repeated the question.

"I just had to shoot Trent Volpone," Tucson said grimly. He added details, telling what had taken place. The other two considered him soberly. "It was him or me," Tucson added.

"He asked for it, I'm thinking," Lullaby said.

Tucson nodded. "I couldn't do anything else. Now I'll have to find somebody to tell Doc Armstrong he'll have an inquest coming up. Or maybe Nirvan sent for him. One way or another it will work out—" He paused, forcing a sheepish smile. "A hell of a deputy I am. I'm forgetting my duties."

"What duties?" Stony asked.

"I plumb forgot that Wonch and Venner are in cells. Unless Volpone fed 'em this morning, they haven't had anything to eat all day."

"My heart bleeds for those two scuts," Lullaby said.

"Mine too," Stony nodded. "Tucson, you won't have time to handle that sort of job."

"Those men have to be fed," Tucson said stubbornly. "That's part of running this job right."

The three procured food from the nearest restaurant, went to the sheriff's office and opened the rear door of the room which led to the jail cells at the back. Here they opened the cells and gave the food to Wonch and Venner. Tucson asked if they wanted to do any confessing, but both swore fervently (thinking Nirvan would soon release them) that they had nothing to do with Sam Dixon's death. Tucson didn't force the issue, but waited until they had finished eating then relocked them in cells.

Ten minutes later the Mesquiteers were in the Brown Bottle. Something was mentioned about feeding prisoners and Johnny Jump-Up said, "In times past I've made a few bucks from the county taking care of that job, Tucson. Beef Yarrow gave me keys to the cells, and I took care of it. I can always get somebody to relieve me here for an hour or so."

"Fine," Tucson said, "you're appointed for the job. We'll arrange about the keys later, though I don't figure you'd better unlock any cells. You can just shove the stuff through the bars."

That settled, the men settled down to bottles of beer. Customers began to depart until only Tucson and his two pardners were left at the bar. It must have been within an hour of sundown when Santone entered. He came boldly in, spur rowels ringing across the plank floor.

"Johnny," Lullaby said sleepily, "your business is picking up at last. Now the enemy is giving you trade."

Santone smiled thinly. "I didn't come here to drink."

Tucson was eyeing the extra gun in Santone's belt, a puzzled look on his bronzed features. "You come to make talk, Santone?"

"A little," Santone nodded. "Consider that I carry a flag of truce in my hand, even if you can't see it."

"What's the joker in the pack?" Tucson asked.

Santone flushed. "There's no joker. What I'm saying is straight talk. I don't hold with Nirvan's methods—"

"Why don't you quit him?" Tucson asked.

Santone shook his head. "I've taken his money—though I should be damned for that—now I'll earn it." He came directly to the point. "Smith, you've raised hell with Nirvan's plans. We don't want you in Manzanita. The town isn't big enough to hold you and me."

"That so?" Tucson queried easily. "What's the alternative?"

"We'll make a game of it, eh?" Santone laughed. "I figure I'm faster than you. Likely you don't believe that. So it's something that should be settled. Do you agree?"

"Could be," Tucson nodded. "What's your idea?"

"Give me time to get back to the Purgatoire. Then you leave here. We start toward each other. Some place along the line we'll come within hitting distance. We each reach for guns when we feel ready. Simple, eh?"

"Very," Tucson agreed. "I'm taking it that Nirvan won't pull any of his slimey tricks in addition."

"Him and me talked that over before I came here," Santone said quietly. "He said he'd keep hands off. It'll be just you and me, Smith. What do you say?"

Tucson said easily, "I've got a feeling I want to stay in Manzanita, Santone, so I'll look for you, once I leave the Brown Bottle. Could be we'll be meeting about midway between here and the Purgatoire. That what you want?"

"That's what I want." Santone nodded crisply. "There's just one more thing." He drew the six-shooter from his trousers' waistband. "I don't want it ever said that Santone took advantage of any man he faced. I'd like you to use this gun. It's a better weapon than yours, Smith. Mine are a matched pair, and you've never pulled trigger on a better gun. They were made to order. The trigger has a feather touch—you can count on it."

Tucson eyed the man. "Feel pretty confident, don't you?"

"I know what I can do," Santone said flatly.

"And you're letting me use this gun?"

"I'd admire for you to do just that, Smith. I want you to have an even break. I don't hate you like Nirvan does. This is just a matter of business with me—but it's as clean business as I can make it."

Both Stony and Lullaby had tried to protest a couple of times, but Tucson had quieted them with a lifted hand. Now he picked up Santone's gun, examined it. "That's one sweet weapon, Santone," he conceded, hefting it in his hand, trying the grip.

"Haven't I been telling you?" Santone said eagerly. "It's a better gun than yours, Smith. It has to be. The factory don't turn out guns like that for the average trade. Will you use it?"

Tucson's eyes narrowed. "I don't know, Santone."

"You figure"—face flushing—"I tampered with the loads? Hell, reload it. Try the gun out—"

"Never had that thought for a minute, Santone," Tucson replied quickly. "Fact is, I trust to your word. But I've never used this gun and I'm familiar with my own Colt—"

"Tell you what—I'll leave it here for you to decide. I can get it later—"

"If possible," Tucson smiled.

"Unless you're a heap better than I think"—Santone answered with a smile of his own—"I'll get it later. Anyway, the matter is settled. I'll be seeing you again shortly." He wheeled toward the door.

"One moment, Santone," Tucson called. "How about a drink before you leave? I'm buying."

A flush of pleasure crimsoned Santone's cheeks. "Don't mind if I do. It's a long time since I've had a drink with your sort of hombres."

He returned to the bar. Johnny, his features troubled, set out bottles and glasses. Drinks were poured. "I sort of wish—" Santone commenced wistfully, then stopped, "Oh, hell, what's the use of wishing now?" He raised his glass. "Here's to a fast draw and a quick death, Tucson Smith."

"*Salud*!" Tucson replied. The two men drank. Lullaby and Stony merely tasted theirs. Santone started for the door again. He paused, turned back a moment. "I'll be seeing you."

"In about ten minutes," Tucson replied, nodding gravely.

Santone disappeared. Silence fell on the room. Johnny spoke, "Of all the cool arrangements I ever heard of—"

"Why not?" Tucson said quietly. "No end is served by a lot of cursing and voicing threats. A man is a fool to go into a gunfight when his temper is on the rise. That Santone is smart—"

"And awfully fast," Johnny said anxiously. "Along the Border he has a terrific rep—"

Lullaby burst out, "Damn, I can't see this. Let me or Stony handle this, Tucson." Stony nodded agreement.

Tucson shook his head. "This is my own job. Can't you see, Nirvan has given his best lead-slinger the chance? By taking down Santone, I put a bad crimp in Nirvan. I'm just glad it's Santone instead of one of the other scuts. Santone, in his way, is on the level. I can't help liking him."

"Don't you get to liking him too much, pard," Lullaby warned.

"I still like myself better," Tucson smiled.

"You going to use his six-shooter?" Stony asked.

Tucson considered. "He called the turn when he said it was a better gun than mine. But I guess I'd better stick to a gun I'm used to. My weapon throws a trifle high. Likely his don't. But I'm accustomed to my gun and it's become habit to compensate when I pull trigger. His Colt might prove a disadvantage."

"I don't like it," Lullaby growled.

"If I'd turned down the challenge how would I look?" Tucson asked. "This is all part of the business of bringing Nirvan to heel."

Both Stony and Lullaby agreed reluctantly. "Do you figure Nirvan will take a hand?" Stony asked.

Tucson frowned. "I don't know," he said slowly. "Anyway, not with Santone's knowledge. Santone is pure killer—some men seem to be born that way—but he's not sneaky."

Lullaby's voice wasn't quite steady. "We—we'll square accounts if—if—"

"Forget it," Tucson said brusquely, "don't count your dead men before they're snatched." He removed his six-shooter, spun the cylinder to see that all was in working order, then shoved it back in his holster. “Santone has had time to get back to the Purgatoire. I figure it’s time I started.”

Silently he pressed the hands of his two pardners. Stony gulped, “Go get him, Tucson. We know you can do it.”

No one had an answer for that, but the others nodded. Tucson stepped out to the sidewalk before the Brown Bottle. The shadows were now long, but instead of the waning day bringing more activity along the street, after the afternoon heat, Manzanita had suddenly gone quiet. Evidently someone from the Purgatoire had passed out word regarding the coming duel. All along the way, men were seen peering from partly shut doors and windows. Two men hurried to remove their horses from hitchracks.

The rays of the setting sun felt warm on Tucson’s back as he moved to the center of the roadway. The last flaming lights were just touching the jagged peaks of the Labajada Mountains. Tucson peered in the direction of the Purgatoire and saw Santone just leaving. As the man moved to the center of the road, he raised one hand in a confident challenge.

Grimly, Tucson answered the signal and advanced to meet him.

XIX

Steadily, Tucson advanced, each step bringing him closer to accurate gun range. There was no faltering, no holding back, in his long even strides. His arms swung at his sides, the hand on the right brushing his holster at each movement. Nor was Santone, in any manner, checking the short choppy steps that carried him closer and closer to the approaching Tucson.

This sort of thing was Santone's game, the sort of thing he lived for. He had been through it countless times before. Countless times? It seemed that many. Eighteen to be exact. Eleven of the eighteen times Santone's opponent had failed to rise from the dust when the fatal shots had been fired. Five times opponents had been disabled. Twice only had Santone failed, in his own estimation, in those meetings; Santone had been outnumbered, though not outdrawn in speed.

Is it any wonder he felt confident? His prowess lay in his fast draw. It was that first shot that counted, and no man had ever beaten Santone to that first shot. Tucson Smith was aware of this. No doubt that Tucson was also fast, but there were many who could match his speed. Tucson was no professional gunfighter. Good, undoubtedly, but he felt in his heart that Santone was faster than he was. Tucson knew he'd have to depend on intelligence, something Santone lacked. It was brain against sheer speed.

Even as he strode along, outwardly calm, Tucson wondered what the end would be. Well, a man could die but once. But which man? Rapidly the distance closed between the two opponents. Santone came on, his demeanor calm, confident. As he drew nearer, one right shoulder hunched a little, his right arm swung a little less.

But forty yards separated the two now. Tucson from the corner of his eye glimpsed faces peering from windows. The street was strangely quiet. Ahead, a number of men were grouped on the Purgatoire's front steps. The sun was nearly behind the mountains now, with the afterglow about to settle on the land.

Thirty yards separated the men now. A novice would already have been throwing lead. Tucson smiled grimly at the thought. Now Santone was smiling a trifle too, an assured, confident smile.

Twenty-five yards lay between them. Tucson shifted his gaze to Santone's gunbutt. Still Santone came on, in no apparent hurry to pull his gun.

Cold sweat beaded Tucson's forehead. No wonder the man had eleven notches to his credit. He waited until his opponent was so close and so occupied with his own draw, that Santone couldn't miss.

Three more yards closed swiftly to two more. Only twenty yards between the men now. Abruptly, Tucson's right hand flashed to his hip!

Fast as he was, Santone was faster. Tucson had never before witnessed anything like that. As though by magic the gun had left Santone's holster.

Tucson held his fire and even before Santone had pulled trigger, threw himself swiftly to one side. Twin bursts of white fire spurted from Santone's gun muzzle.

For just a moment his view was partially obscured by the black powder smoke rising from the exploding weapon. He only saw Tucson moving sidewise and took it for granted his two shots had struck Tucson.

Then Santone made his mistake. With the smoke swirling before his eyes, he leaped forward to throw in quick finishing shots, but his gun was raised too high.

Too late he realized that Tucson hadn't fallen, but was crouched low to the ground, knees bent, six-shooter leveled for action. And in that moment, Tucson released his fire. An instant too tardy, Santone tried to swing his gun-muzzle to bear on Tucson, but the maneuver was useless. He felt slugs ripping through and through his body, tearing bone and flesh and muscle.

Santone paused, stretching to tiptoe, both arms flung high, the gun falling from one hand from which all strength seemed to have departed. Twice he whirled around then pitched forward on his face. He was laughing now, a throaty bubbling laugh as he struggled to rise. Gamely gritting his teeth he managed to achieve a sitting position just as Tucson came running in.

"It's all over, Tucson," he said thickly. His hands fumbled for Durham and papers. Somehow he managed to fashion a cigarette, while Tucson gazed on in amazement. Tucson stooped by his side and saw the answer in Santone's eyes, already taking on a glazed look.

"My God, you're fast," Tucson whispered in admiration. He put one arm about Santone's shoulders to support the man.

Santone swayed back. Again that throaty bubbling laugh. "Fast, did you say?" he mumbled, "fast? Hell, I'd give all my speed for that stunt of yours. Brains beat speed. I never did have brains." He fumbled for a match.

Tucson struck one on his thumbnail, held the flame to Santone's cigarette. The man drew gratefully on the smoke. Tucson knew he couldn't last much longer. The cigarette dangled loosely from Santone's lower lip. His gaze wasn't focusing right.

"Would you shake hands with me, Tucson," he panted, the words spaced far apart. "I'm not holding this against you—just glad it took a good man to finish me. I've been—just dyin'—to see you—in action." An attempt at the bubbly laugh. "Good joke, eh? Take my guns, Tucson. They're even—good enough for you—"

"I'll take 'em, Santone. Gladly. And thanks—"

There was excited yelling along the street now. Tucson knew that Lullaby and Stony would be here any instant. Beyond that, he was unconscious of the sudden wave of activity along the thoroughfare. A hundred feet distant, a low-browed, dirty-looking individual had just poked a Winchester barrel from the open window of a deserted adobe hut.

Tucson wasn't aware of that. He was feeling regrets for the fast-departing life of Santone now. Suddenly the man stiffened with an effort and Tucson could just make out the words: "I—damn' nigh—forgot," Santone gasped, "look out—for—Hugo Riley—rifle. Ain't sure but—Wetzel dropped something—reckon Nirvan lied—to me—"

Tucson let Santone quickly to the earth and spun around, moving quickly to one side. At the same instant a rifle cracked. A leaden slug kicked up dust and gravel where Tucson had been stooping but a moment before.

Santone began to cough. A strange rattling cough. "Dammit," he fought for breath, "get cover. I can die alone—"

A second shot cut the bandanna at Tucson's throat. Tucson half rose to his feet. He saw Stony and Lullaby racing toward an adobe hut some distance away on the opposite side. Both men were firing as they ran. A third slug whistled harmlessly over Tucson's head. "Will you go?" Santone groaned.

"I'm staying with you, Santone," Tucson said grimly. "My pards are taking care of that dry-gulcher. I doubt he'll fire again."

But Santone was too far gone to understand. "Brains beat speed," he murmured drowsily. "You're white, Tucson, white clear through." Abruptly his head rolled to one side and he died.

Tucson rose, stopping only to pick up Santone's gun, then dashed toward the adobe hut, where the firing had already ceased. Stony and Lullaby were just emerging. They leaped to meet him, seizing his hand. "That rifle hombre in there?" Tucson asked.

"He'll do no dry-gulching again," Lullaby said meaningly, adding, "I don't know which of us got him through that window. He was finished when we broke in."

"What now?" Stony asked.

"Stony, you slope down to the undertaker's. I want Santone taken care of prompt. And there's the other fellow in that adobe."

"Why you so concerned about Santone?"

"Maybe if you'd faced him, talked to him,

you'd know how I feel, Stony. He was plenty game. I want him to have a decent burial. Lullaby, see if you can locate Doc Armstrong. Warn him that he'll have more than one inquest coming up—"

"Where you going?" Lullaby wanted to know. "The Purgatoire?"

He glanced quickly along the street, but not a person was seen in front of the place. Tucson said, "I'm heading for my office. There'll be a report to write on this business. The Purgatoire? We'll leave that until a little later."

"I've a hunch," Stony said, "that Nirvan has learned a lesson."

"Maybe," Tucson said grimly, "and maybe we'll have to teach him one tonight."

XX

Night had fallen over Manzanita, though here and there groups stood along the sidewalks discussing the excitement of a few hours before. Now that they'd learned Nirvan wasn't invincible, people were speaking up more boldly and were getting ready to give their new deputy the backing he deserved. Tucson, with Lullaby and Stony, returned from late suppers and entered the Brown Bottle to find the saloon filled with customers. Johnny was perspiring profusely as he worked to satisfy thirsty demands.

"Business seems to be picking up," Tucson commented.

"Not only seems—*is!*" Johnny said, grinning.

"To what," Lullaby drawled, "do you ascribe this unusual impetus toward the mart of hard liquor and hangovers?"

Johnny winked, and nodded toward Tucson.

A man at the end of the bar spoke, somewhat sheepishly, "I reckon I can answer that question. Sometime back, Nirvan sent out word that anybody trading here might be in for a mite of trouble. Seems he had us all buffaloed for a spell, but the last couple of days seems to prove that Nirvan isn't as strong in Manzanita as he thought he was. The new deputy and his two pards has sort of made this town ashamed of itself."

"That's the talk," another man put in. "I guess we were all sick of Nirvan's crooked games, but now the time's come to assert ourselves—"

"Nirvan don't get any more of my trade," from a third. "He's had things his own way for too long. Johnny, if you'd just remodel your place and make it larger and get in a few games and some girls, you'd run Nirvan out of business."

"Maybe so," Johnny nodded. "But I reckon I'll leave the running out to somebody else."

The evening wore on. Tucson and his pardners strolled about town but everything seemed quiet, with the exception of the Purgatoire, which by this time was fairly jumping with activity.

They glanced at the place as they strolled past. "Think Nirvan will close at midnight as you ordered him to?" Lullaby asked.

"I haven't the least idea," Tucson replied, "but I reckon to be on hand to see what action he takes."

"Not alone, you won't," Stony said quickly.

"We're going," Lullaby put in, dolefully, "but there goes my night's sleep shot all to hell again. I'll be glad when this town's gentled down. I've a hunch Nirvan may be mad and refuse to close."

"Not mad—insane is the word." Tucson laughed softly.

"You're going to call his bluff if he tries to stay open?" Stony asked.

"That's the way I'm figuring," Tucson said quietly.

Lullaby drew a long sigh. "Just as I suspected. There's more trouble coming and no rest for the weary. Now that's settled, let's go get some coffee and cherry pie. If I'm going to be busy, I've got to have more sustenance."

Stony jeered at him, but quickly followed Lullaby's lead to the restaurant, with a thoughtful Tucson trailing behind.

It was nearly eleven-thirty when Tucson and his companions entered the Purgatoire. The place was running full blast. At the bar, two bartenders were working feverishly to attend customers. At the rear, the orchestra played for perspiring dancers who revolved and capered about the floor, bumping into each other. Across the room from the bar were the games of chance—if chance it could be called in the Purgatoire—faro, dice, the wheel, roulette, blackjack, poker. Odd tables here and there held poker games, or bottles for those too inebriated to stand at the bar.

Curses, wild laughter, ribald oaths mingled with the clicking of poker chips and the droning tones of gamblers as they raked in suckers' hard-earned money. Cigar and cigarette butts littered the floor. The odor of liquor, stale tobacco and sweat filled the smoke-clouded room. Above swung the kerosene lamps in brackets, flames jumping in the chimneys from the vibrations of so much activity.

Tucson and his companions pushed through the crowd, Lullaby wrinkling his nose. "Something's mighty odoriferous."

"The whole place needs renovating," Tucson nodded.

"Said renovating," Stony put in, "should be done with a few of Samuel Colt's lead cleaners."

They proceeded across the room to the opposite wall, brushing off three of the dance-hall girls who'd been quick to spot them, now that the orchestra had stopped for a minute.

One girl in particular fastened herself on Tucson. She was the one he'd seen in the Purgatoire earlier that day. "Aw, come on, Mister Deputy, just one dance. The sheriff wasn't as shy as you. I had to fight Beef Yarrow off every time he came in here."

Tucson smiled gravely at the girl. "There's a mite of difference between Beef Yarrow and me. At that, I can appreciate Yarrow's good taste in some directions."

The girl flushed. "Now you're just—what is it the cowboys say—? you're just hoorawing me."

Lullaby and Stony pushed on to inspect the games. Tucson glanced about the room. Neither Nirvan or his henchmen were in sight. They were probably all in Nirvan's office.

The girl pouted. "Well, if you refuse to dance with me, will you buy me a drink?"

Tucson extracted a silver dollar from his pocket

and handed it to her. The girl looked at the dollar, then up at Tucson. “Won’t you drink with me?”

Tucson read something more than a desire for a drink in her eyes. He gazed steadily at her a moment, taking in her cheap prettiness, beaded eyelashes and rouged cheeks. Her short spangled skirt just reached below her knees. The girl met his survey honestly.

Tucson nodded. “I’ll drink with you. Order what you want.”

“Let’s find a table.” She led the way to a round-topped table covered with circular liquor stains. Tucson waited for her to seat herself, then sat down. The girl raised her voice to one of the bartenders. “Tony-y-y! How about a little service?”

The barkeep caught the words through the steady roar of voices and nodded. Within a few minutes he appeared to take the order. Tucson ordered a couple of glasses of wine. The barkeep returned shortly, tray in hand. He placed the glasses on the table, received the money and pushed back through the crowd.

Tucson’s hand went to the glass but before he could raise it to his lips, the girl exchanged it for her own. Tucson said, “Any particular idea back of that move?”

“I just wanted you to know that your drink didn’t have any little white powder in it.”

Tucson smiled. “Thanks. What’s your name?”

She told him her name was Lucile. Tucson asked, “Are little white powders in general use here?”

Lucile looked scornful. “As if you had to ask. I could tell today when you came in that you knew what sort of place this was. And the way you took care of yourself proved it—”

“I seem to remember you cried out. Thanks for the warning.”

The girl shook her head. “You already knew what was going on.”

Men were milling all around. In the event Nirvan did glance out of his office, he wouldn’t be likely to see Tucson and the girl seated at the table, hidden below the heads of the crowd. They drank their wine. Tucson offered a second drink which was refused with thanks. Tucson said, “Lucile, you wanted more than a drink. What’s on your mind?”

“Nirvan, mostly,” the girl said bitterly. “He’s a beast. After you shot Volpone today, he flew into a rage. Later, he took some of his rage out on me. Look at this.” She extended her bare arm which had black and blue marks on it, then she laughed suddenly. “Don’t think I brought you to this table to listen to my hard luck tale. Look here, you came tonight to see that Nirvan closed by midnight, didn’t you?”

“Suppose I did?” Tucson asked warily.

“I heard you tell him this afternoon. He’s going to be ready for you by twelve o’clock.

He'll pretend he didn't know it was closing time. He'll agree to close up. Just as the customers are leaving, a fight will break out. Bullets will fly wild and one of them will have your name on it—by accident, of course."

"Interesting," Tucson said. "I'm glad to know that. But why do you tell me?"

"Because," the girl snapped, "I want to see somebody settle Matt Nirvan's hash. He's rotten, clear through."

Tucson frowned. "In that case, why do you stay here?"

Lucile laughed scornfully. "You don't know Nirvan. He hardly ever pays us all he should. It takes money and friends to be able to leave a town you hate." She lighted a cigarette and passed it to Tucson. "Take a drag, Mister Smith, and act careless. That other bartender is watching us. Tony is all right. Fact is, I'm going to marry Tony, if we ever get enough money together to get far away from here. But I don't trust that other bartender."

Tucson took the cigarette and laughed as though the girl had told him some joke. He inhaled deeply of the smoke, then passed the cigarette back to the girl. She rose, shaking out her short skirt. "I've got to get back to the dance floor before Nirvan comes out of his office and sees me talking to you. I just wanted to give you the tip, that's all."

"Wait a minute," Tucson said. She seated herself again. Tucson pulled some bills from his pocket and passed them under the table. "Here, take this. You and your Tony get out of town as fast as you can. Get his ear, tell him what you want to do, and leave right now. You can get a rig at the livery to carry you to the nearest railroad station. Get your clothes, and slip out fast. You won't be noticed going in this crowd. Give Tony my best wishes. *You've* already got 'em."

"But—but, I can't take money from you." The girl's lips quivered, her eyes filling. "I'm not asking pay for what I told you, Mister Smith—"

"That's why I'm giving it to you." Tucson's voice took on a rougher tone as he rose from the table. "Go on, kid, beat it. I don't want any arguments." Without waiting for her reply, he rose and left the table, leaving her in her seat.

A moment later as he threaded his way through the crowd, he heard her voice, "Tony-y-y! How about a little service over here?"

Tucson stopped to watch. He saw Tony look up and nod. In a few moments he came to the table where the girl sat. She whispered to him. Tony's face lighted up, then he returned to his bar. Lucile hurried up to the second floor. Scarcely five minutes had elapsed before she descended, carrying a small satchel. Tony left his bar, took the girl's arm, and the two hurried from the Purgatoire.

“And that’s that,” Tucson smiled. “Love seems to hit ever’body but Tucson Smith. Well, I’m wishing those two all the joy they can get from the life ahead of them. They should be some distance off before their absence is reported to Nirvan—fact is, I aim to keep Nirvan too busy to think of them for a spell.”

He crossed to where Stony and Lullaby were watching the games, then signaled for them to join him. The two pushed through the crowd to his side. Stony said disgustedly, “These games have as many crooked twists to them as a sun-fishing bronc.”

Lullaby smiled. “I sort of like these games—especially the galloping dominoes. I’m forty-nine bucks to the good.”

“You crooked tinhorn,” Stony accused.

Tucson laughed. “How’d you work it, Lullaby?”

Lullaby said lazily, “The minute I touched those cubes I knew they weren’t meant for me to win with. Pretty crude dice, but good enough to catch suckers. But when in Rome I burn Roman candles. If crooked dice are the order of the day, I’ll cooperate. So I introduced a pair of my own—and took ’em out before I quit, forty-nine bucks ahead. That dice gambler is still trying to puzzle out what happened at his table.”

“Lullaby, you should be ashamed of yourself,” Tucson chuckled. “Cheating the Purgatoire. You—carrying crooked dice!”

"It's a pair of bones I took from a tinhorn down in Tombstone one time," Lullaby said placidly. "I just hung on to 'em for such emergencies."

Tucson, in a low voice, told the two of the plan related to him by Lucile, about the fake fight to be staged, so that he could be downed by an "accidental" bullet. ". . . And you two know what to do," he concluded. "So let's get busy. It's past twelve now."

The three pushed their way to the bar. The bartender snapped, "What's your orders?"

"My orders," Tucson said, "is for you to quit serving and announce that the Purgatoire is closing for the night."

"Yeah," the barkeep sneered. "Who says so?"

"You know the laws of the town. I'm enforcing those laws."

The barkeep looked uneasy. "Oh, sure, Mister Deputy, didn't recognize you at first. You see, I ain't had no orders from Matt Nirvan."

"You'll take orders from me."

"I'll have to send word to Mr. Nirvan." He turned around, "Hey, Tony, go tell Matt that—hell, where's Tony? I—"

At that moment Nirvan appeared from his office. None of his gunmen were present. "Oh, hello, Smith," he greeted, working his way through the crowd. "I was just coming out to close up. I'll attend to it right away." He raised his voice, "Everybody out, folks! Closing time!"

Then, back to the barkeep. "No more drinks to be served, Sleeky."

The customers started to leave, many of them reluctantly. Gradually, the roulette wheel slowed to a stop. Cards and chips were put away. The gamblers began covering their equipment. Within a short period all of the customers had departed except for four hard-bitten looking individuals who were arguing loudly at the far end of the bar. Nirvan nodded good-bye to the bartender and said to the four, "Come on, you hombres, the law says you've got to move on. We're closing. Here's the deputy. Talk to him if you don't like it."

They swung around, glanced irritably at Tucson, then returned to their bickering, without paying any attention to Nirvan—as they had been paid to do. Their voices rose louder, two of them appearing to take sides against the other two. Their hands were dropping near holsters.

"By Gawd!" one of them swore. "It ain't so, and I can—"

"I tell you it is, you ornery skunks—"

"Who's a skunk—?"

"Both of you bastards—"

"By geez, you take that back—!"

The fake fight had started. The four men were spreading out a little, that certain slugs might have no difficulty reaching Tucson Smith. Nirvan had backed off, pleading with the men to quiet down and leave peacefully. They paid him no attention.

Tucson glanced at Lullaby and Stony, gave them an imperceptible nod.

Nirvan cried, “Men, men, stop it! You’ve got to leave. Deputy Smith says I have to close, and that means you—”

One of the four pseudo combatants growled over his shoulder, “ ’T’hell with the law. This hombre called me a skunk and—”

“I ain’t takin’ it back,” answered another. “If you want action I stand to show you plenty.”

“See?” Nirvan appealed to Tucson. “They won’t listen. What can I do?” It was so palpably false that Tucson could scarcely refrain from uttering a scornful laugh.

“I don’t know what you’d do, Nirvan,” Tucson snapped, “but I’ll show you what I can do. . . . Come on, Lullaby—Stony!”

XXI

The four men were just pulling guns preparatory to staging the fake fight, when Tucson and his two pardners charged in, guns in hands. Tucson struck the first man he reached a glancing blow with the barrel of his six-shooter. The fellow staggered back with a howl of pain. Lullaby and Stony closed in fast, gun barrels swinging right and left.

Sharp startled yelps rose on the air as the four scattered to avoid the swinging barrels. Two of them crashed to the floor. A third staggered weakly against the bar. The fourth man flung his arms in the air. "I'll get out," he growled. "I don't want any trouble with the law."

"You should have thought of that before," Tucson said sternly. "All right, get out while you can take a whole skin with you. And takes your three pals along at the same time. If you feel so tough, the four of you can shoot it out in the street. But don't ever again try to slip a fake fight over on me."

"Fake fight! Fake fight?" Nirvan protested. "What do you mean, Smith?"

"You know damned well what I mean," Tucson snapped.

"I don't understand what you're hinting at—" Nirvan began.

"I'm not hinting."

Nirvan shrugged. "You got me all wrong, Smith."

"Nobody could get *you* any other way. You're wrong all through."

Nirvan's pasty features tightened. "I don't want any trouble with you, Smith. Since you've taken charge of these hombres who tried to start a fight here, I'll let you get rid of them, while I count my night's receipts. You'll have to excuse me while I go get my money sack." He wheeled about, went back to his office and closed the door behind him.

"Keep your eyes peeled," Tucson spoke to Lullaby and Stony, then turned and gave his attention to the four would-be bad men. All four were on their feet now, ranged, frightened, along the bar. Tucson laughed sarcastically. "Cripes! You four are certainly tough. I should jail you as public nuisances, but there's no use putting the county to the expense of feeding four bums. Get out of Manzanita within one hour or I'll take you in on a vagrancy charge. Now get!"

The four lost no time making themselves scarce. They left the doorway at a staggering run and disappeared in the street. Manzanita never saw them again.

Tucson laughed softly. His gun was still out as were the guns of his companions. All three were half expecting Nirvan's door to open again and were ready for anything such an opening might bring. But apparently Nirvan didn't want more trouble this night. He didn't reappear and Tucson neglected to take into consideration that there might be a rear door in the office, leading to the alley that ran back of the Purgatoire. They waited ten minutes more at the bar, then Tucson said, "I reckon we'd better slope, pards."

As they were leaving, the door of Nirvan's office opened and the man's head showed momentarily in the opening. "Good night, boys," he said mockingly. "Glad to have you drop in any time."

"We don't need your invitation, Nirvan," Tucson snapped. "I expect to be dropping in right along—until you've dropped out."

Nirvan's door slammed with a bang.

Tucson and his pardners stepped into the street. It was dark all along the way now. Here and there a square of yellow light showed from a building. The stars added slightly more illumination. Light still showed from the open door of the Purgatoire, throwing the three into bold relief as they walked down the steps and swung to the right on the sidewalk.

Stony was a little ahead. "I'm out of makin's, Tucson. Let me have your Durham, will you?"

"Sure." Tucson reached for the tag dangling from an upper vest pocket. "Here you are—"

The sharp crack of a rifle interrupted the sentence. From across the street a livid tongue of flame licked through the gloom. With a sudden groan, Stony stumbled and went to his knees. A second shot followed the first!

By this time, Tucson and Lullaby had seized Stony and dragged him to the shelter of a nearby watering trough. Stony braced himself on one arm, reaching for his gun, as Tucson and Lullaby cut loose with their six-shooters in the direction from which the Winchester shots had come.

"That first shot was meant for me," Tucson grated. "Damn those scuts, if they've hurt Stony bad—"

"I'll be all right, Tucson," Stony whispered, wincing with pain.

Again the rifle snarled, sending a leaden slug whining over the heads of the three. This time Tucson had seen the flash of fire, coming from a shadowed passage between buildings across the roadway.

Tucson stole a quick glance over his shoulder. All appeared to be the same at the Purgatoire as it had before. There was some excited yelling farther down the street, but no one came near. Tucson's gun was empty now. He punched out the shells and reloaded. Another rifle slug buzzed viciously past his head, followed closely by still one more slug.

"There's two rifles hid over there," Tucson said to Lullaby. "They've got more reach than we have. You stay here and see that no harm comes to Stony. Keep your eye on the Purgatoire too. I'm crossing over to try and stop those rifles."

"But—" Lullaby commenced a protest that came too late.

Tucson was already leaping to his feet and sprinting toward the other side. Straight into a hail of fire he ran, but he was moving in zigzag fashion and proved a difficult mark to hit. He was two thirds of the distance across when the firing ceased and he heard the sound of running feet.

Reaching the opposite side, he plunged into shadows between two dark false-fronted stores. Here he paused to listen. Someone was running along the alley at the rear of the buildings. Tucson leaped forward, but just before entering the alley, he dropped to his knees and peered around the rear corner of one building.

From the gloom farther along came a stab of flame. A bullet splintered a corner of the building above Tucson's head. He jerked erect, thumbed two swift shots from his six-shooter. He knew he had missed for again he caught the sound of running feet. He reloaded the two empty gun chambers while he again jumped into pursuit.

From the darkness ahead came the crashing roar of a forty-five. One of the men must have completely emptied his rifle. In the momentary flash from the gun, Tucson glimpsed Bronc Rabideau's face.

Abruptly, Tucson uttered a hoarse groan,

and dropped to the earth where he lay without movement.

"I got him!" Rabideau's voice shook with excitement. Tucson lay very still, eyes striving to pierce the gloom. He heard footsteps approaching. Gradually, Rabideau took form in the darkness, as he hobbled into view, movement still somewhat handicapped by his wound.

Tucson laughed grimly, came to his feet. Jets of living flame spurted from his forty-five. There came a high-pitched yell of anguish, then Rabideau plunged down, thrashed about a moment, and lay still, a few yards beyond.

"Like hell you got me," Tucson said grimly. He raised his voice, "Hey, you other coyote. I'm waiting. Come and get it!"

Lances of orange flame replied to the challenge. Two bullets flew high. A third came dangerously close. "Hell!" Tucson grunted, "I might's well go after the skunk."

He started along the alley, triggered two swift shots. He wasn't expecting to hit anything, but he was working to keep his opponent back until he could come close enough to make certain of his firing. The other man was just two buildings away now. In the excitement of the moment, Tucson had forgotten Rabideau. He took another step and suddenly went down, tripping over Rabideau's lifeless body.

For a moment the impact stunned him. His gun

went flying from his hand. From the darkness came an exultant exclamation of triumph. It was Shive Otis's voice. The man was dimly outlined in the darkness. Tucson struggled half erect, hand fumbling to find his gun. His fingers closed about the butt. He raised the weapon in a quick shot that missed, but it held Otis off a few seconds.

Cautiously, Otis lifted the Winchester to his shoulder for a finishing shot, the hammer clicking as Otis drew it back. Tucson raised his Colt gun, pulled trigger. The hammer of the gun snapped down on an empty shell!

XXII

Rifle lead whined past Tucson's head, almost scorching his temple. Again he thumbed back the hammer, pulled trigger, and once more the hammer fell on an empty shell. The first time he thought the gun had misfired. Now he realized the cylinder was empty. His ears caught the sound of Otis levering another cartridge into the Winchester.

A hoarse growl of triumph rose in Otis's throat. He came two steps closer, making certain he wouldn't miss the helpless Tucson again. Then Tucson acted. Without rising, he hurled his empty weapon at Otis's head. Too late the man saw it coming. He tried to dodge that brief glint of flying steel he'd seen, just as the gun struck the side of his head.

Tucson leaped to his feet, closing in on Shive Otis. Half stunned from the blow of the flying six-shooter, Otis staggered back, slipped and went to one knee, the rifle flying from his grasp. At the same instant, Tucson seized him. Snarling like a wounded coyote, the man rolled over and over, carrying Tucson with him, battling with every ounce of strength to shake off the grip of the fighting deputy.

Tucson hung grimly on. Otis was a much

heavier man than Tucson and for a few moments seemed to have the better of the struggle. He bit, clawed, cursed, striking out with savage blows. Twice he succeeded in pinning Tucson beneath him, his hands clawing for Tucson's throat. And twice with a mighty effort, Tucson hurled clenched fists to Otis's head, breaking the man's powerful grip.

Both men were panting heavily now. Tucson's cleaner life commenced to give him a slight advantage. Otis's breath was coming in painful gasps. Bringing his last ounce of strength into play, he flung Tucson to one side. With the Winchester gone, Otis still had his six-shooter in holster. Catlike, Tucson scrambled back to prevent Otis drawing the weapon, but he was too late. Otis's fingers had already curled about the butt. Just in time, Tucson seized the man's wrist. With all the force at his command, he bent the gun backward . . . just as Otis pulled trigger!

There came a savage roar, a blinding flash of orange fire—so close that the exploding powder burned Tucson's face buried in Otis's chest. But the leaden slug had plowed upward through the bottom of Otis's jaw. Tucson felt the man go limp under his hands. Otis's fingers uncurled from the gunbutt, and he fell back, without even a groan.

Tucson waited a moment, tortured lungs drinking in fresh air, albeit tinged with the odor of powder smoke. Otis hadn't moved. Tucson felt for a heartbeat. There wasn't any. He got wearily to his feet, searched in the darkness for his six-shooter, found it and reloaded the depleted chambers. Then, striking matches, he examined the bodies of Rabideau and Otis. Both were dead, no doubt of it.

"Me, I'm sure lucky," Tucson muttered. His heart was still pounding. Halfway back to the spot where he'd left Stony and Lullaby, he met Lullaby running toward him. Tucson said, "Stony—?"

"He's taken care of. Lot of people there. I sent for Doc Armstrong. But what happened to you?" Tucson told him as they strode back to the street. Lullaby expressed some awe at Tucson's luck. "You don't need to tell me I'm lucky," Tucson said shortly. "If I hadn't got more than my share of breaks, there'd been a new deputy in Manzanita." He was scratched and bruised.

There was quite a crowd around when they got back to Stony. Someone had furnished a blanket and the wounded Stony was stretched out on the walk, his head pillowed on the folded blanket, smoking a cigarette. "Still cheating the undertaker, eh?" he said weakly as Tucson bent above him. "It sure sounded like an arsenal had gone up in smoke."

"You hit bad, Stony?" Tucson asked anxiously.

"I don't reckon so," Stony answered. "I'm just feeling lazy for a few minutes. Lullaby says I'm struck low down on the right shoulder. Can't say it hurts much, though?' Somebody in the crowd passed in a flask of whiskey and Stony was given a stiff jolt from the bottle and this appeared to brighten him considerably. Tucson told him of the fight with Otis and Rabideau.

A horse-drawn buggy came rolling up, drew to a stop and Dr. Armstrong jumped out. He was a small, stockily-built man with a bald head, blue eyes and a cheerful manner. He spoke to Tucson and Lullaby, ordered the crowd back, and in the light from lanterns someone had brought, made a quick examination. "Sorry I couldn't get here sooner, but from the message Joslin sent, I thought my rig might be needed to carry Stony. It took a mite of time to hitch up." He was still probing around the wound. Stony jumped suddenly. "Hurts, eh?" from Armstrong.

"Hell, no," Stony forced a grin. "I thought you were aiming to tickle me."

"I'll do my tickling with this." Armstrong held up a hypodermic syringe. "That's the trouble with you cow folks. You try to laugh off your hurts. Don't you know this could be serious? Don't be so danged cocky. Suppose I was to tell you you were at death's door?"

Stony forced another grin. "In that case, I'd have to ask could you pull me through." He winced as the needle shot home. In a few moments he gave a long sigh of relief.

Armstrong said, "Now if you fellers will help me get Stony to the seat of my rig—"

"Hey," Stony cried in alarm. "I'm all right. I don't have to ride any place."

"That's what you think," Armstrong said tersely. "I've got to take you to my office and probe out that bullet."

Despite Stony's protests, he was taken to the doctor's house and placed on a long table. Lullaby and Tucson remained until the leaden slug had been removed and Stony, with the aid of an opiate, had fallen instantly to sleep. Armstrong assured Tucson and Lullaby that all was going well, and providing Stony's wound didn't become infected he'd be around in a couple of weeks or so.

Tucson and Lullaby made their way back to the main street. Tucson sighed. "Well, that makes two of us to do the work of three."

"We'll just have to work a little harder, Tucson. What's the next move?"

"I'm heading for the Purgatoire, right now," Tucson stated, "and place Nirvan under arrest. I hope he resists."

"Good. But on what charges?"

"Murder and a few other things—"

"How about proof—?"

"I'm forgetting that for the present," Tucson said grimly. "That's why I'm hoping he'll resist. It might save a lot of court expense." Lullaby pointed out that Nirvan would likely have Wetzel and Black Payette with him. Tucson said, "I haven't forgotten them either. You ready?"

"Cripes," Lullaby drawled, "I'm waiting for you to catch up."

XXIII

Tucson and Lullaby strode up the steps and entered the Purgatoire. Now only one lamp burned in the big, deserted barroom and gambling parlor. The men's guns were already drawn, ready for instant action. Beneath Nirvan's door a strip of light showed. Lullaby and Tucson listened. Low voices reached their ears. Tucson's hand went to the knob of the office door. The knob turned but the door was locked. Within, the sounds of voices stopped abruptly. There was a moment's silence, then Nirvan's voice: "Who's there?"

"Tucson Smith. Open up, Nirvan!"

"What for? I've been asleep. You woke me—"

"No use lying, Nirvan! We heard voices in there. Open *pronto*!"

"What for?" Nirvan stalled, not troubling to deny he wasn't alone. "We're busy right now."

"Plotting more skulduggery, eh?" Tucson snapped. "Nirvan, Otis and Rabideau are finished."

From behind the door came Nirvan's sarcastic laughter. "Heard you'd had a fight with those two. I didn't have anything to do with that, Smith. I'm not responsible for what they did—"

"That's your story, Nirvan. I'm placing you

under arrest. Do I have to break down this door?"

There came a long pause. Tucson could hear men moving about within the office. He and Lullaby moved back from the closed door, standing at either side, and just in time.

Wham! Wham! Wham! Three leaden slugs came ripping through the wooden panels at a point where Lullaby and Tucson had been standing but an instant before. Lullaby's face flushed with sudden anger at such treachery and he raised his gun to reply. Tucson signaled him to hold his fire. Lullaby nodded he understood. He and Tucson stood like graven images, not making a sound now. Within the office, all was silence. The crack of light under the door faded to darkness. Nirvan had extinguished his lamp. Still Tucson and Lullaby didn't move. Five minutes passed, drifted into ten, and then a quarter hour. Lullaby and Tucson hadn't made a sound.

Finally, from within the office came a low whispering. Another five minutes passed, then ever so gently came the turning of the doorknob. Tucson and Lullaby stood as before, scarcely breathing. The door opened another inch. Tucson nodded to his pardner. Two guns roared almost simultaneously as Tucson and Lullaby cut loose.

There came a long-drawn groan and the sound of a falling body. The door started to swing back. Instantly it was slammed shut. From inside the office guns started to explode. Slug after slug crashed through the panels, without finding marks. Up on the balcony that ran around three sides of the room, a couple of doors opened quickly and were as quickly shut again. Several of Nirvan's employees slept up there.

Lullaby leaped across the room, overturned a big round table on its side, then called to Tucson. The two crouched behind the table. From this point they could watch the balcony as well as the door of Nirvan's office.

"You keep an eye on the balcony," Tucson said. "I'll watch Nirvan's door. Maybe we can smoke those scuts out. I don't figure there's much to fear from that balcony, though. Those people up there aren't the kind to risk their lives. Just some girls and tinhorn gamblers."

Lullaby nodded and sent a slug crashing against an upper corner of one of the balcony doors. Meanwhile, Tucson had emptied a cylinder through Nirvan's door and started to reload. "We'll make it hot for those coyotes, even if we don't hit anybody," he chuckled. By now, Nirvan's office was starting to reply to the firing. It wasn't long before the door panels took on a sieve-like appearance. Powder smoke floated through the big room. Two bullets chipped the table edge behind which Tucson and Lullaby were shielded. Other slugs flew harmlessly about the room.

The advantage lay with Tucson and Lullaby.

They could at least see the door through which they fired and feel sure of coming fairly close to their opponents, while the Nirvan faction were more or less shooting blind. A few frightened faces of townsmen had peered in at the open doors at the entrance, but quickly dodged back out of sight when one of the slugs from Nirvan's office went screaming through the entrance to the street.

Abruptly, Nirvan's voice called through a lull in the shooting: "I give up, Smith! We'll come out. There's just me and Wetzel. Payette is finished."

"Come out with your hands high," Tucson yelled. "Leave your guns behind."

There was a moment's silence. With his feet, Tucson made walking sounds. That did it. A veritable hail of lead ripped through the door. Again, Nirvan had played false, thinking to lure Tucson within gun range. Bullet after bullet sprayed the room at all points, as Nirvan and Wetzel made a last desperate attempt with their guns to find Tucson and Lullaby and mow them down.

Lullaby and Tucson crouched close to the floor, waiting for the hail of lead to stop. From a room on a balcony, came a woman's frightened scream. Tucson felt certain she'd not been hit. Leaden slugs were still raining through the now splintered door. One of them struck a shelf of bottles back of the bar. An odor of whiskey filled the room and mingled with the odor of black powder smoke. Lullaby chuckled coolly, "Nirvan is sure having one hell of a time, wrecking his own joint."

"He'll tire after a time, then we'll get him," Tucson replied.

"Unless he has some luck and gets us first—"

Crash! One of the flying bullets had struck the sole remaining light suspended from the center of the ceiling, splashing oil in all directions. Instantly the Purgatoire was plunged into darkness, except for a remnant of burning wick that had fallen to the floor.

"By God, he'll set the place on fire," Tucson yelled. Regardless of the bullets still flying around, he leaped from behind the shelter and started toward the burning wick. But the movement came too late. There came a sudden rush of flame as the fire caught the spilled oil and swept across the floor. The flames licked along the bar, caught. The dry wood began to snap and crackle. Smoke ascended in clouds.

Tucson lifted his voice: "Fire! You folks upstairs had better come out! Nirvan, your place is on fire and going fast. It's your last chance! You and Wetzel had best surrender!"

"Go to hell!" came Nirvan's defiant answer, and sent another slug ripping through the door.

Doors along the balcony banged open. Nirvan and Wetzel had ceased firing now, but still refused to open their door. The flames roared along one side of the barroom. The heat grew swiftly, as dry wood caught and was consumed with the fierce swiftness of burning paper. Down the stairs leading from the balcony, came a line of women in wrappers and hastily dressed frightened men. All had their hands in the air. Some of the girls were whimpering.

"Go on!" Tucson yelled up to them, "get out as fast as you can. We don't want you people."

Within a couple of minutes all had reached the safety of the open air. Tucson and Lullaby had backed against the front wall now. The heat was almost unbearable. Perspiration streamed down their faces. Lullaby panted, "If we stay here we'll be roasted."

"I can stay as long as Nirvan," Tucson stated grimly. Again he raised his voice, "Better come out, Nirvan. You're trapped!"

A long shelf of whiskey bottles came down with a crash behind the bar. There came a gigantic puff of flame, as the raw whiskey added fresh impetus. Unbroken but overheated bottles began to explode, hurling glass fragments in all directions. Tucson said dumbly, "Lord, I'm a stupid buzzard!"

"What do you mean?" Lullaby panted.

"Maybe Nirvan got out by the rear."

"We'd have seen him."

"I don't mean by that back door we see from

here. Could be there's a door from his office too. I'm going to see."

Followed by the protesting Lullaby he plunged through the choking smoke. The riddled door of Nirvan's office was still locked. Tucson threw his weight against the door and sent it crashing loose. The door hung from one hinge. Tucson pushed it open and stepped into the office, gun at ready. Then he lowered the gun.

Behind him there came a renewed rush of flames as a fresh draught was created by a small open door leading to the alley. The flames sent a lurid light through the office. Previously that open door had been hidden by a tall cabinet which had now been pushed to one side. There was no sign of Nirvan or Riker Wetzel. The leaping flames threw into plain view the dead body of Black Payette, sprawled face down on the floor.

"They're gone!" Tucson exclaimed ruefully. Followed by Lullaby, he plunged into the alley where stood a small barn. The barn door was open. Within, three horses stood in stalls, neighing nervously. Two stalls stood empty. Lullaby led the horses outside and tethered them some distance off. Then they returned to the rear door of the Purgatoire. The interior of the building was a raging inferno now. The flames crackled and roared as the sun-baked wood blazed as though oil-soaked. Tongues of red and yellow light licked through the open door. The roof caught and the roaring was redoubled.

Lullaby and Tucson made their way around to the street. Already a crowd had gathered. Long lines of men were engaged in passing buckets of water to throw on the adjoining buildings. Fortunately there was little breeze and the fire burned almost straight up. The buildings on either side of the Purgatoire were scorched, but little other damage was done. For a short time longer the flames roared, the roof fell in, blazed fiercely, then commenced to die down. In an hour all danger of other buildings catching had passed. In another hour the Purgatoire was a heap of smoldering embers.

Several men remained to throw water on the smoking ruins, though most of the crowd went home. To those who inquired, Tucson explained briefly how the fire had started. Within a short time, he and Lullaby were ready to leave. Dawn was streaking the eastern horizon with orange banners, as they walked wearily along the street. Lullaby said, "Everybody I talked to seemed to think that Nirvan and Wetzel would never show their faces here again."

"What do you think?"

"I don't figure Nirvan will give up that easy. He's got too much at stake."

"My idea too. He's still got property in town, and he owns the Lazy-Y Ranch—regardless how he got it. I've a hunch he'll lay low until he can cook up some other scheme. Meanwhile, we may get a few days' rest. Lullaby, there's two cots in my office. What say we turn in?"

"That's the first good idea I've heard in some time," Lullaby yawned. "Lead on, Deputy. I'm in your custody."

XXIV

A week slipped past with nothing untoward happening. Nothing more had been heard from Matt Nirvan. Ringbone Tilford, Johnny Jump-Up and several others were firmly convinced that Nirvan had left the country for good. But not Tucson. Tucson said, "You mark my words, that snake will return, and when he comes back he'll be dragging a small chunk of hell along with him. He won't quit until he's finished me—or I've finished him."

Tucson had made a trip out to Nirvan's Lazy-Y Ranch, but found it deserted, except for a dirty old cook who was still living there.

"I dunno what Matt had in mind, or where he's went to," the old cook grumbled. "He sent some sort of message to the foreman, and everybody pulled out right *pronto*, leavin' me all alone. Dunno where they went. Matt owes me some wages or I'd quit."

Tucson mounted his horse and rode off, leaving the old fellow still grumbling. He was convinced the cook knew nothing of Nirvan's movements. Manzanita had proved to be unusually peaceful since Nirvan's departure. Nirvan's saloons in town were permitted by Tucson to operate so long as they obeyed the laws. He had no authority to close them, otherwise.

Stony's wound was healing fast and he was on the mend. Ringbone Tilford had heard of the wounding of Stony and two days after he had been shot, Tilford came in with instructions from Louise to the effect that Stony, if able to stand the jolting of a wagon, was to be brought to the Wagon-Wheel for recuperation. This proved a solution for Dr. Armstrong's problem, as the doctor had had to give up his own bed to Stony.

For a while after that Armstrong had made a trip to the Wagon-Wheel every day, to check on his patient. The bandages needed changing at regular intervals. When Louise offered to take care of this, the doctor was grateful and complimented the girl on her skillful nursing ability. So far as a quick recovery was concerned, it was the best thing that could have happened to Stony. Tucson frowned slightly when he saw how Stony's eager gaze followed the girl's every move. Stony was eager to get out and about again, but this, Dr. Armstrong discouraged. "Wait another week, Stony. Even now it wouldn't take much shaking around to reopen that wound."

A mile below the Wagon-Wheel, in a shady grove of cottonwoods, on Cottonwood Creek, Stony and Louise had gone one morning for Stony's first outing away from the ranch house, since the night he'd been wounded. He was still rather shaky, and Louise had had Ringbone Tilford hitch up the buckboard for the trip. The two had seated themselves in the shade, alongside the cool flowing stream. The girl had brought along a book and was reading aloud, but it is doubtful if Stony heard the words, as he gazed at her in dumb adoration. Noontime approached and Louise suggested she go back to the ranch and pack a lunch.

"Why not let me make the drive with you?" Stony asked.

"Bad for the wound. You just rest quietly. You have tobacco and matches. I can leave here, pack a lunch and be back within the hour."

"It'll seem like ten hours," Stony protested.

"Thank you, sir"—Louise made him a mock bow—"but I long ago learned not to believe in cowboy flattery."

"I'd like a chance to prove it's not just flattery," Stony said boldly.

Louise laughed, then a slight frown formed on her forehead as she mounted to the seat of the buckboard and gathered the reins in her hands. The buckboard rolled off followed by Stony's adoring gaze. When it had disappeared over the first rise, Stony settled his back against a tree trunk and started to manufacture a cigarette.

Three quarters of an hour slipped by, then an hour. A few minutes later came the sounds of distant shooting. For a moment, Stony thought nothing of it, then when the firing continued, he rose slowly to his feet. "Damn funny," he scowled. "I thought maybe that was Posthole Turner or one of the other boys shooting at tin cans, but come to think of it, all the hands are out on the range this morning. Only Ringbone and Sloppy Wuther are there."

His brow creased with concern as he walked slowly up the first rise of land that led to the Wagon-Wheel. By the time he'd reached the top he was panting from the unusual exertion, realizing now he was weaker than he'd thought himself to be. His worry mounted. Louise should have returned by this time. He pushed on with dogged determination. Twice he had to drop down for short rests. Finally he reached a point where he could look down on the roof tops of the Wagon-Wheel buildings.

He had hoped to see the girl on the way back, but there wasn't a movement to meet his anxious gaze. Stony strained his eyes toward the ranch house. He could see the buckboard standing in the shadow of the house, but no sign of Louise. Neither could he see Tilford or the cook moving about.

Stony's gaze shifted toward the west and a groan of dismay parted his pale lips, as he sighted a body of riders traveling fast toward the foothills of the Labajada Range. One of the riders looked like a girl, and two men were riding close as though she were a captive.

Somehow, Stony staggered the remaining distance to the Wagon-Wheel buildings where a gory sight met his eyes. Ringbone Tilford lay dead in a pool of coagulating blood, gun still clenched in his stiffened fingers. At the doorway of the bunkhouse, sprawled Sloppy Wuther, half in, half out of the building. A shotgun lay a few feet away. Both barrels had been fired, but the old cook had been riddled with outlaw lead. Some yards off, Stony found two more lifeless bodies, both strangers to him, but the dead set features looked vaguely familiar: Stony felt sure he had seen the two hanging around the Purgatoire before it had burned.

Cursing feebly at his weakness, Stony started toward the corral at a stumbling run. Three times he fell down before he reached the enclosure. His wound was throbbing painfully again, but he went doggedly on, his mind dwelling on the crimson slashes that had been cut across the foreheads of Tilford and Wuther. But what had happened to Louise? That question was quickly answered by a note fastened to the top bar of the corral. Stony jerked it off and read:

> *To Tucson Smith and the Town of Manzanita—Give me gold money the value of my properties in and around Manzanita, and Louise Dixon will be released unhurt. I'll send word later where the money can be sent. Don't*

attempt to follow me, or what happens to the girl will be on your own heads. I mean business! Matt Nirvan.

Stony groaned, while a cold rage ran through his body. The fiends! No telling what might happen to Louise. It seemed to require a giant's strength for Stony to procure a saddle and get it across a pony's back, but somehow he accomplished it. Luckily the horse proved docile and there was no spirited bucking as Stony hauled his body on its back. His first inclination had been to take up Nirvan's trail, but he had sense enough to realize his strength might not hold out. Blood was seeping from his wound again. The bandage beneath his shirt had started to stain.

He drove in his spurs and the horse swung toward the trail to town, almost unseating Stony. Three miles slipped past beneath the swiftly running hoofs. Stony's bandage had begun to loosen by this time; the throbbing pain was almost unbearable. At times Stony rode with his eyes closed, leaving the pony to find the way. By this time the horse was in a lather, but Stony refused to let it slow pace. It was sheer will-power that kept him upright in the saddle now. Fortunately, he wasn't forced to maintain that reckless speed all the way to Manzanita.

Tucson and Lullaby, on the way to see their wounded comrade at the Wagon-Wheel, spotted him coming from some distance off, riding at breakneck speed. Tucson yelled as Stony approached closer, and the horses were brought to a halt in a swift scattering of sand and gravel. In an instant, Tucson and Lullaby had dismounted, just in time to catch Stony as he slipped sidewise from the saddle.

"Stony, Stony! What's gone wrong?"

Stony extended the note Nirvan had left, then mumbled out the tragic story, before fainting away. Tucson went white. He spoke quick orders to Lullaby who'd stood cursing grimly while Stony's story was related. Lullaby nodded and Tucson vaulted into his saddle, riding like the wind in the direction of the Wagon-Wheel, intent now on picking up Nirvan's trail before it became too cold to follow.

Once Tucson glanced back over his shoulder and saw Lullaby helping Stony into the saddle. Despite Stony's protests, Lullaby was taking him in to Dr. Armstrong. Tucson pounded on.

XXV

It was the second day following Louise Dixon's abduction. Across a waste of sand and alkali, Tucson Smith rode, grimly following a trail that led across desert country. Here and there he passed small clumps of creosote bush and stunted sage. Cactus dotted the desert wastes at some points. Once a straggly mesquite met his wind-and-dust-burned eyes.

Tucson had arrived at the Wagon-Wheel and after moving into the bunkhouse the bodies of Tilford and Wuther, had left a note for the return of the other hands to tell them what had happened. Then he had retightened his saddle cinch and loped out to pick up "sign" on the outlaw band. It wasn't long before he had located the direction taken by Nirvan and his men—some dozen of them, Tucson had decided, after closely scrutinizing the hoofprints in the earth.

The trail had led him into the winding recesses of the Labajada Mountains. For hours Tucson had stuck with the trail which led always south. Nirvan was making for Old Mexico, no doubt about that. Tucson cursed savagely at the thought of a girl like Louise Dixon taken into Mexico by an unprincipled scoundrel of Nirvan's caliber. Twice, Tucson had lost the trail where it crossed a wide stretch of hardpan. Each time he had found himself winding up in blind canyons, and had been forced to retrace his way, thus losing precious time before rediscovering Nirvan's trail.

Toward morning, after traveling all night, he had been forced to halt and rest his pony, while he snatched a few winks of sleep. Then once more he had saddled up and pushed on. When he crossed the border into Mexico he wasn't certain, but he knew from the look of the country that he had left United States to his rear. In time he had emerged from the southern reaches of the Labajadas to find a long stretch of desert country ahead. Night had again descended and with it came the so necessary rest for both man and horse. The only water they'd found had been at a small alkali-tainted water hole on the fringe of the desert country they were now crossing.

Both Tucson and the horse were covered with a fine coating of gray dust which lay like a mantle across their forms and penetrated eyes and throat and nostrils. He had drawn his bandanna up across his mouth and nose, but it served but feebly to obstruct the sharp penetrating alkali. Hour after hour they moved on beneath the scorching rays of a sun like molten brass. By now he was on the right track again. Every so often he'd spy hooftracks that the sirocco-like wind hadn't yet erased from the sandy surfaces.

Toward evening the pony got into gradually

rising terrain. More mesquite trees began to appear and grew taller. In time, Tucson came to piñon-covered slopes, and judged he was in the foothills of the Poco Torvo Mountains. Huge blocks of sandstone and granite began to bar his way from time to time and he'd be forced to twist this way and that, as he followed the dim trail. At spots the way was cluttered with broken rock, over which the weary horse slipped and stumbled.

In time, Tucson reached the crest of a hill and again started a long gradual descent. Here, however, there seemed to be a well-worn trail between precipitous rock walls. The descent into the gulch was steep, but fairly wide. Tumbled heaps of boulders were piled at either side. To the left of the trail was a tiny stream of shallow water, that became deeper as Tucson proceeded. Here both man and horse relieved their thirst and the animal was allowed to crop a bit of the coarse grass that grew nearby. Then they went on, once again, Tucson thinking, This trail seems well-traveled. Perhaps there's a small settlement nearby where I can get food.

It became dark in the gulch. Tucson glanced up between the high rock walls on either side. Far above, he could see a narrow strip of blue sky, but he realized sundown wasn't far off. Ahead, the way began to widen. In a few minutes he'd be traveling across more open ground. He was just passing a jumble of high cluttered rocks when it happened:

Too late his ears caught the swift *swish* of a thrown rope, quickly followed by a repetition of the same sound. Two hempen loops dropped about his shoulders, tightened, pinning his arms to his sides. The next instant, Tucson was jerked bodily from his saddle and thrown heavily to the rock-strewn earth. For a moment he was stunned by the sudden fall. Then as he struggled to his feet, Nirvan and two other men came scrambling down among the rocks and hurled themselves on the struggling Tucson. Their first move was to get his gun.

For a few minutes, Tucson fought like a madman before the strength of the three overcame him. A minute more and he was securely bound. One of the men tried to catch Tucson's horse, but the animal, striking out with forefeet, reared and eluded him. As the man leaped back out of danger, the pony swung about and dashed frantically back up the gulch.

"Let the horse go, Steppie," Nirvan ordered. "We got Smith. That's good enough luck for one day." He stood above Tucson, lying helpless on the earth. "Damn you, Smith. I finally got you where I want you. It's your finish, you know."

Tucson was breathing heavily but he held his voice as steadily as possible. "No, I don't know, Nirvan. This game isn't finished yet. I'd be willing to lay even money you'll be all through before many hours have passed."

Nirvan laughed confidently. "You can't run any more bluffs on me, Smith. Things have swung my way now. You made good time sticking to our trail, I'll admit, and I was glad to see you alone. We kept an eye on you all across the desert—me and the boys from my ranch—Turk, and Steppie—"

"Where's Louise Dixon?" Tucson demanded.

"About three miles up ahead. I sent her on to camp with Riker Wetzel and the other boys. Don't worry, she's safe—so far. Which reminds me, I'd better go see to her. Wetzel considers he's got a way with fillies, and I wouldn't want any harm to come to the girl. I want her in good condition when Manzanita pays over money for her release. Of course, if Manzanita tries to stall me off, I won't be responsible for anything that happens—"

"No decent man expects a coyote to be responsible," Tucson said contemptuously. "You—" The sentence was interrupted as Nirvan kicked Tucson brutally in the ribs. A sharp pain ran through Tucson's side. The two men known as Turk and Steppie exposed tobacco-stained fangs in evil grins as they saw Tucson wince.

Nirvan jeered loudly. "Bring him along, boys."

Tucson was lifted to his feet and half carried, half dragged the remainder of the way out of the gulch. In time a broad open spot beside a stream was reached. Here a small fire burned. At one side were picketed the three horses of Nirvan and his two men.

Nirvan mounted. “Reckon I’ll drift ahead and tell Riker and the girl what we’ve hooked. Be back in a little while, Steppie, you and Turk watch that hombre close. He’s tricky.”

“He won’t get away,” Turk said confidently.

Nirvan rode off through a clump of cottonwoods and disappeared. The sun dropped from sight. Night fell almost instantly. Steppie and his companion set about making supper. Turk threw mesquite roots on the fire, then got busy with frying pan and coffee pot. Tucson lay where they’d dropped him, some yards from the fire. At times, silence fell between his two captors and he could hear the cool sounds from the nearby stream. His thirst increased. His side ached where Nirvan had kicked him. After a time he asked for a drink of water. Steppie rebuffed him, but Turk was a trifle more humane. “What difference does it make?” Turk argued. “Smith gets his finish in the morning, anyway.”

“Suit yourself,” Steppie shrugged. “I can’t be bothered.”

Turk gave Tucson water and fed him some bacon and bread. He ended up by holding a tin cup of hot coffee to Tucson’s lips. Tucson began to feel a trifle better. He sank back and tried to sleep. The time might arrive when he'd need all the strength he could get.

The hours passed. Steppie and Turk began to wonder why Nirvan didn't return. Midnight came. Tucson slept fitfully. When the two men rolled into blankets and began to snore, Tucson tried to burst the ropes that bound him, but his efforts were without avail. Again, he fell asleep. Once during the night he awakened. The fire had died to glowing embers. Then he fell asleep again.

It was almost daylight when he next awoke. The eastern sky was aglow with rose lights. Tucson struggled to a sitting position, just as Nirvan came loping on his horse through the trees. Steppie and Turk were still asleep when Nirvan dismounted.

"Damn you lazy buzzards!" Nirvan snarled. "Come alive." He glanced at Tucson and an evil grin twisted his lips. Steppie and Turk crawled from their blankets, rubbing their eyes and yawning.

Turk stretched. "Thought you was comin' back last night."

"I figured that way too. I went to that clump of Mex houses and got what I wanted. It's on my saddle. Good and sweet and thick, too. Then I made for the camp. Wetzel wasn't there. When I found him, him and me had some words. He's getting too big for his britches, and had moved the camp seven or eight miles farther on where he'd found a small shack. He'd been getting pretty familiar with the girl too. It was that mostly we argued about. He didn't touch her none, but I don't reckon we'd best leave him alone with her too long. We'll get busy and join the others as soon as possible."

He led his horse to the stream to drink, while Steppie and Turk packed their belongings. When he returned, Steppie announced, "We're all ready, Matt."

"Fine, I'll help. The molasses and pickets are on my saddle."

Tucson lay quiet, wondering what they planned to do. He felt sore and stiff. His head ached. His limbs were so cramped that even when his bonds were removed he could scarcely lift his arms or move his legs.

Nirvan chuckled evilly. "Wait until you learn what a fine little party we're aiming to fix for you, Smith. I'm only sorry I can't stay and enjoy the show. I'd enjoy hearing you beg for mercy. But you can thank Wetzel for making it necessary for me to leave. I've got to keep an eye on that snake. Howsomever, I'll be thinking about your finish every minute. Get busy, boys."

Tucson's bonds had been completely removed by this time. He was lifted to his feet, but was so stiff he could take only a faltering step. While he speculated what they intended to do, Steppie and Turk half carried him across the stream, the blood rushing back to cramped limbs making each movement painful. Nirvan followed close behind, his gun barrel boring into Tucson's back.

The men splashed calf-deep through the stream, dragging Tucson along. Reaching the opposite bank he was thrown down. Here, Steppie and Turk proceeded to strip off his clothing. Boots, socks, shirt, underwear, trousers . . . Then, Tucson saw what they intended to do and his heart sank.

Only a few yards away was a mound of earth nearly three feet high, with a diameter greater than the length of a man's body. Holes, leading to tiny tunnels, dotted the mound. An involuntary groan burst from Tucson's lips. The mound was an anthill!

A hill of millions of red ants. Red ants three-quarters of an inch in length. Ants, always ravenous for food.

A rage welled in Tucson's breast. His fist shot out, striking Turk in the face, but the blow lacked force. In another instant both men were on him, holding him down. Tucson fought as well as he could for a moment, but his limbs were too stiff to respond promptly. The movements helped his circulation but such relief came too late.

While Turk and Steppie held him prone, Nirvan smeared molasses over Tucson's naked body. Nirvan chuckled as he worked. "I'll bet you know all about being staked out on an anthill, don't you, Smith? The Death of a Thousand Deaths, the 'Paches called it. What's the limit a man can last? Twenty minutes, isn't it? A fine meal for the ants. I remember seeing a man once that spent ten minutes on an anthill. He was rescued before the ants finished him, but he might just as well have been left there. His mind was gone complete. I understand a man's mind begins to slip in the first seven minutes. The ants have a habit of boring into every orifice in the body—throat, mouth, ears, nostrils. . . ."

Tucson struggled furiously, but the men held him down. "It doesn't take long for those ants to bore in, Smith. You'll squirm all right—and scream! The molasses will help attract the ants to you and give 'em an appetite. But you'll have one consolation—no man ever lasts more than twenty minutes."

Turk spoke to Nirvan while he and Steppie held Tucson prone. The sun was above the horizon now, blazing down with fierce intensity. Nirvan quickly drove long picket-pins into the mound. Still fighting, Tucson was carried over and spread-eagled atop the anthill. His arms and legs were stretched out and fastened with rawhide thongs to the picket-pins. Tiny crawling things with sharp jaws were already investigating Tucson's bared chest.

Turk and Steppie worked swiftly, but even before they had finished, the ants were at work.

Tucson felt sharp bites along his legs. He stiffened and tried to pull loose. Nirvan laughed at his efforts. "Scream, Smith! Damn your hide, why don't you scream?"

Turk and Steppie rose to their feet, brushing off ants, swearing. With Nirvan they crossed the stream and mounted their horses. A moment later they loped their horses out of sight, leaving Tucson to his fate. Tucson groaned and writhed. The ants were working all over his body now. From the distance came a last mocking laugh from Nirvan as the drumming of horses' hoofs died away.

XXVI

Tucson tried to hold still beneath the torture. Then it became unbearable. Ants swarmed over his body now. He kept his eyes tightly shut. Like a myriad tiny burning coals the savage little insects attacked. Tucson spat and blew and strained. They clustered in his hair and ears. Violently, he shook his head from side to side until his muscles rebelled. The ants only returned to the attack with renewed ferocity.

It seemed ages since Nirvan and his two men had departed. Actually it was less than two minutes. Tucson groaned and writhed, as thousands of tiny jaws, working through the molasses, clamped down on his burning flesh. His body stung like fire, and he arched his body, twisting as far as his bonds would permit.

Again he started shaking his head. Sharp needles drove into his scalp, gnawing relentlessly. A scream rose to his lips. Doggedly, he choked it back. He wasn't noticing the heat of the sun now. Compared to the Death of a Thousand Deaths, that would be a blessing. But the heat combined with the thousands of gnawing ants was more than a man could bear and still retain his sanity.

For a moment, Tucson thought he was going crazy. Then, driven to desperation by the torture, he strained more fiercely at the rawhide thongs that held his arms. He tugged and grunted and swore. Veins on his forehead stood out like twisted knots. Sharp pains pierced his ribs where Nirvan's kick had landed.

Tucson gritted his teeth and tried again. His biceps swelled, became rigid. His arms went steel hard. The ants were driving him now to a point almost beyond human endeavour. It required willpower to do what Tucson Smith was doing, fighting on while still retaining his sanity.

Suddenly, he felt one of the picket-pins give slightly. He strained more fiercely. Again the picket-pin moved. A mumbled exclamation burst from Tucson's lips. Another last effort . . .

The pin jerked loose! Now his left arm was free, the pin dangling at the wrist. Tucson twisted on his side, worked at the other pin. That too was jerked from the sandy earth. Ah, good! He brushed the ants from his face and bent to loosen his legs. The pins were in deep, but they were gradually coming loose. There, that's one! Now the other leg . . .

In another instant Tucson had rolled frantically from the top of the mound and scrambled erect. Picket-pins still dangling from his limbs, he made a dash for the stream, brushing off ants by the hundreds as he ran. One wild splash and he was prone in the water, ducking his head beneath the stream, submerging his whole body beneath the rippling depths. Clusters of ants went floating off on the water, as Tucson lifted his head and ducked again several times beneath the surface. Some of the little insects hung on with the tenacity of bulldogs. These he slapped to death.

After a time he rose from the stream, entirely free from ants. His body was covered, red as fire, with tiny bites. It would be days before his skin regained its natural color. He released the rawhide thongs and picket-pins from his limbs and stepped from the water to get his clothing which Nirvan and his men had left scattered about near the bank of the stream.

"If Nirvan had had sense enough to drive those pins in at a slant, instead of straight in, I'd never have made it," was the thought that passed through his mind. "And solid earth would have been harder than that mound already loosened with tunneling. I sure am lucky."

He dressed quickly. The exertion and the cold water had removed much of the stiffness from his limbs, but his ribs still pained. He swore softly at his empty holster. It didn't look as though he could do much with neither gun or horse. After a moment's thought he decided to start back, on foot, through the gulch, in the hope of finding his pony. Then, he could resume the search for Nirvan and take a chance on finding a gun some place along the way. He took one final look at the anthill where the ants were scurrying around, busy as ever. Tucson shuddered. "Yep, I sure had luck on my side."

He splashed on across the stream and reached the opposite side. The thought occurred to him that Nirvan might return, expecting to find Tucson's bones picked clean. "Yes, I'd better drift away from this spot as fast as I know how. I'd be helpless without my Colt gun."

He pushed on up through the gulch, walking as fast as his aching side would allow. By now he was fretting angrily at the delay occasioned by the absence of a mount. Suddenly from behind him, he heard a shout. Glancing over his shoulder, he saw Nirvan, Turk and Steppie, quirting their horses in swift pursuit. Nirvan had found it impossible to resist the temptation to return and gloat over whatever he found left on the anthill.

Tucson swore under his breath. Such a break! Well, he'd not stand still and wait for them to recapture him. He broke into a run. At any instant he might see his pony up ahead. Scrambling, slipping, panting, he moved along the uneven floor of the gulch. From his rear came the roar of a forty-five and a leaden slug ricocheted from wall to wall, but he was still too far distant to make an accurate target. A second shot whined overhead. The riders were gaining now.

"Cripes!" Tucson gasped. "That was getting closer. I'd better look for shelter."

He darted behind a big boulder. Several chunks of loose rock lay near at hand. Tucson stooped swiftly and seized a rock in each hand. "Maybe I'm due for a finish," he said grimly, "but I sure would like to get close enough to mash in Nirvan's skull with one of these pebbles—"

And then, from the other end of the gulch came another pounding of horse's hoofs. There came the sharp crack of a Winchester rifle! Tucson caught the savage oath that Nirvan ripped out. He and his men were already turning their ponies, starting to retreat. Again came the bark of the Winchester. Tucson saw Steppie throw up his arms and plunge from the saddle. Now, Nirvan and Turk were pounding their mounts over the head in a desperate effort to escape the range of the rifleman.

Tucson stepped out from behind his boulder. Then he gave a yell of pure joy. Loping swiftly toward him through the gulch rode Lullaby Joslin. Joslin was guiding his pony with knee pressure as he operated the Winchester. But his remaining shots were wasted. Nirvan and Turk disappeared around a bend in the gulch. Steppie's horse with its riderless saddle, trotted after them a moment, then stopped and fell to cropping some grass growing between rocks.

Lullaby waved as he thundered past at breakneck speed. Tucson saw him draw rein beside the wounded Steppie and dismount. Lullaby stooped above Steppie for a minute and talked to him. Then he rose and remounted. A few moments later he was stepping down at Tucson's side. Their hands met in a firm clasp.

"Am I glad to see you, Tucson! I—My Gawd, what happened to your face. Looks like you had a whiskey rash."

"Ants," Tucson said briefly. "They started to eat breakfast at my expense. Is Steppie finished?"

"Steppie? Oh, that hombre I dropped. Yeah. The shot got him through the lungs. He said something about Wetzel and Nirvan having an argument. Then he died, cursing Nirvan. But what all's happened to you, pard?"

"Plenty." Tucson told the story of the happenings since he'd left the Wagon-Wheel. Lullaby's face went hard when he heard about the anthill torture. ". . . And then," Tucson concluded, "I was heading up this gulch to look for my horse when Nirvan and those other scuts came riding after me. I was certain glad you arrived when you did. Any more help on the way?"

"I sure hope so. I lit out to find your trail as soon as I got Stony to Doc Armstrong's. What? No, Stony's all right. Doc says he just set himself back a week or so. Anyway, I rode straight back to the Wagon-Wheel. I saw the note you left and added another note for the boys to come riding and look for beans—"

"Beans?"

"I found a burlap sack and a half, full of beans in the cookhouse and took them with me. Every so often as I rode I dropped some of them white beans along the way. Once I'd picked up your trail, I scattered more beans. Hope the birds haven't stolen 'em. At places your trail was right hard to read sign on. My beans run out complete just as I reached this gulch. 'Course, I was right careful of the beans and just dropped 'em in the hard places to see—"

"What next?"

"Just as I entered this gulch I saw your horse and picked him up. Had him with me, but when I heard those shots I dropped him off and come on. I saw you tearing up the gulch with Nirvan after you. Brought your rifle along too, as well as Santone's guns. Figured you might need 'em—"

"Lullaby, you think of everything. Give me those guns quick."

Lullaby produced the twin six-shooters from the roll back of his saddle. Tucson drew a long sigh as he dropped one gun into his holster and stuck the other in his waistband. Lullaby said, "I'll carry your rifle until we pick up your horse. What? Yes, I brought plenty of ca'tridges for both six-shooters and Winchesters. My pony was sure carrying a load for a spell. Before I left I told Johnny Jump-Up to send word to all the ranches. I imagine that some of the gang that held the meeting of the Terrible Twelve will be coming along—but how soon, I don't know. Do we wait for 'em to show up?"

"Wait nothing," Tucson exclaimed. "Let's get my horse, then you and I will take out after Nirvan and his skunks."

"Will your side stand the strain?"

Tucson nodded. "Better than I can stand the strain of Louise Dixon in Nirvan's hands," he said, hard-voiced.

Lullaby nodded. "Hop up behind me and we'll go find your pony."

A short distance farther up the gulch they saw Tucson's pony, contentedly cropping at the sparse foliage that grew along the stream. Tucson climbed into his saddle, got his rifle from Lullaby and shoved it into the scabbard beneath his left leg. Drawing Santone's six-shooters, one by one, he examined them to make certain they were loaded. Then, wheeling his pony, he said, "I'm ready, Lullaby."

The two riders went clattering through the gulch, moving as fast as the uncertain, rocky footing permitted.

XXVII

It was getting along toward eleven that morning when Tucson and Lullaby first sighted the Nirvan camp. The two riders had followed the stream as it twisted around trees and boulders, before finally reaching a long gradual slope, cluttered with rock and yucca trees. At the foot of the slope stood a small adobe hut. Men were moving around the house, seemingly unconcerned about the approach of Tucson and Lullaby.

"I'm damned if I like this," Tucson frowned. He and Lullaby drew their horses to a walk. "Seems like Nirvan would have made some preparation for our arrival. I wouldn't want to go down there and ride right into a trap."

"Maybe he thinks the two of us wouldn't come alone, when he's got a gang. You said he had around a dozen men."

"Yes. But there aren't more than four or five in sight down there. I don't see anything of Nirvan or Louise."

Lullaby reached for his rifle. "Well, two of us can't tackle them alone, but there's nothing says we can't make it hot for them from up here." The horses moved a few steps farther down the hill. Lullaby brought the rifle to his shoulder, taking careful aim.

"Pretty long range," Tucson commented.

"Yeah, I realize it . . ." Even as he spoke, Lullaby tightened his finger about the trigger. The Winchester cracked sharply.

A man near the house leaped frantically to one side. The others dashed for shelter. Rifle smoke was whisked away on the breeze. In an instant there wasn't a man to be seen. Lullaby swore. "Dammit! I missed!"

"Bet you scared him spitless, though," Tucson chuckled, lifting his own rifle.

Spat! A rifle bullet flattened itself against a rock, close to Tucson's head, followed by a perfect rain of slugs that went whining past Tucson and Lullaby. Lullaby's horse screamed and reared in pain. The animal's knees doubled under it when it came to earth, and it went rolling over and over down the slope, Lullaby just managing to extricate his feet from the stirrups in time. He was afoot now, with Tucson yelling for him to jump up behind.

It was all a mad blur of tumbled rock, dust and the barking of guns. Lullaby had gone down, but was up again, limping slightly. Heedless of lead whining all around, Tucson spurred to Lullaby's aid.

"Go ahead, spur like hell," Lullaby snapped, catching Tucson's stirrup. Tucson turned the horse and the two dashed back up the slope.

"You hurt?" Tucson called to Lullaby sprinting at his side.

"Not none—just twisted my ankle a mite," Lullaby panted.

Tucson didn't take time to reply. He had spied a natural formation of rocks that would form a perfect barricade, and was now heading for it as fast as his horse could carry them there. A couple of seconds later they arrived. Tucson flung himself from his horse, then he and Lullaby dashed for the shelter of the rocks. Reaching the spot in safety, they dropped to hands and knees, breathing hard.

"Damned if we didn't walk right into a hornet's nest," Tucson said. In front of them rose a long outcropping of granite ledge. Behind were two boulders, each the size of a large room.

"Where in the devil did those shots come from?" Lullaby said.

Tucson gestured off to the right, where a second heap of jumbled boulders had provided an excellent ambushing spot for the Nirvan faction. Lullaby lifted his head for a quick look, then ducked down again. Instantly the tops of the Nirvan rocks were fringed with ragged white fire. Lead spattered wildly all around.

"Keep down, you locoed idiot," Tucson grunted. "Think I want to be stuck here all alone?"

"I'd sure like to take a crack at those skunks if I hadn't lost my Winchester when the dirty scuts dropped my horse from under me," Lullaby snapped wrathfully.

The two men sat back and took stock of their situation. They were about halfway down the long hillside, and held the commanding position over the adobe shack at the bottom. At the same time, the Nirvan men held the advantage behind their rock shelter, which lay slightly higher up the hill than the position held by Tucson and Lullaby, though they were off to one side.

For a time the Nirvan men continued to waste lead. Now and then a bullet would ricochet dangerously near Tucson or Lullaby, but for the most part they were in a pretty safe spot. The sun blazed down unmercifully as time passed, with only desultory firing now. Lullaby became impatient. "Dammit! I wish we could do something."

"Not much we can do," Tucson pointed out. "We're outnumbered and those coyotes can starve us out, if they see fit. I wish I had a canteen of water—or just one drink."

"Me, I've been trying to forget about water," Lullaby growled.

"Stick a ca'tridge in your mouth," Tucson suggested. "It'll help some. I figure there's a couple hours more of daylight, then sundown. When it gets dark we'll try to make a sneak for it. My horse is only a short distance off where he wandered looking for grass—"

"Mine isn't far off either," Lullaby said with grim humor.

"But mine's alive."

"We might as well be dead. We'll never reach your bronc."

The two rolled cigarettes and lighted them. Tucson grew restless. "Jeepers! I'm getting tired of this."

He rose boldly to his feet, then as quickly dropped down again as a slug whined past his cheek. "Now who's the idiot?" Lullaby demanded.

"We both are," Tucson smiled grimly, "for getting cornered like this. Those hombres are sure keeping a bead drawn in this direction. But I found out what I wanted to."

"What's that?"

"There's a couple of hombres wandering careless-like down near that adobe. They figure we're afraid to try anything—"

"Well, aren't we?"

"Sure. But we're going to try anyway. Lullaby, those hombres on the hill back of that rock ledge haven't had much lead poured at them. Try throwing some forty-fives their way. I doubt if you'll hit anything, but maybe you can keep 'em under cover while I try a shot with the Winchester toward those hombres near the adobe."

Lullaby nodded. "Anything is better than layin' here, dying of thirst. Let me know when you're ready." Tucson signaled him to start.

Lullaby drew his six-shooter and elevating it

above his rock shelter sent a steady hail of bullets toward the Nirvan faction. Meanwhile, Tucson had raised up and leveled the rifle across the top of the ledge. His finger closed about trigger, tightened . . .

A sharp, whip-like report cut through the booming of Lullaby's six-shooter. Tucson grunted with satisfaction as he saw his target go sprawling on the earth. Instantly he levered another cartridge into the Winchester's chamber, sent a random shot flying at a second man. There came a yelp of pain as the second man too went down!

"Good Lord," Tucson exclaimed. "I got two of 'em. No! That second hombre is crawling away. He's hit hard though. There's nobody left in sight down there now."

He wheeled and commenced pumping lead toward the rock barricade of the Nirvan men. In a moment his rifle was empty and he sat down to start reloading. "Reckon I didn't hit much," he said cheerfully, "but it sure relieved my mind some to talk back a mite."

Stung to action by the flying lead of the two, the Nirvan men again started shooting. Guns thundered and roared. Flying slugs filled the air and ricocheted wildly about. Suddenly Lullaby grunted and sank back to earth.

"You hit?" Tucson exclaimed anxiously.

"Sort of—not bad, I reckon." Lullaby was

pressing one hand against his side. It came away, splotched with crimson. He forced a cheerful grin. "Guess I just lost some skin from my ribs. Now we both got bad sides to contend with—"

"I'd damn nigh forgotten mine. Let me see that wound."

Tucson ripped open Lullaby's shirt, then the undershirt. An angry red furrow lay just below Lullaby's arm pit. Tucson took their bandannas and made a bandage. "That'll hold for a spell. It's like you said—a mite more than a scratch."

The enemy firing had died to silence again. On an abrupt impulse, Tucson stood erect, rifle at shoulder, triggering and levering as fast as he could. From behind the enemy stronghold came a sharp cry of pain. One of Tucson's slugs had evidently found an opening between rocks. As he dropped down to reload, a perfect fusilade of firing whined above his head, some of the bullets striking the rock at his rear.

"They sure got us pinned down," he commented and started to roll a cigarette. He lighted it, thrust it in Lullaby's mouth and manufactured a second for himself. His face was sweat lined through the powder grime.

Lullaby, somewhat pale, was reloading his forty-five. He said, "I sure wish some of the boys would show up, but even with those beans I dropped the trail would be hard to follow. And there's not much more daylight left—"

At that moment a wild yell broke out from the Nirvan barricade. Tucson leaped to his feet in time to see the Nirvan men fleeing down the slope for the safety of the adobe hut.

"I'll be damned!" Tucson snapped. Seizing his rifle he poured shot after shot at the running men. Two of them stumbled and dropped. Then, over the top of the hill, came the staccato pounding of horses' hoofs. Posthole Turner, followed by Curly Folsom, King Cole and some twenty other cowpunchers came sweeping down the slope. Tucson gave a wild yell of greeting. He and Lullaby waved their sombreros in joy.

"Here's where Nirvan gets accounts squared!" Tucson cried. "Squared in gun smoke or I'm a pie-eyed idiot!"

The riders were already halfway down the slope, guns out. They tore past, faces grim, spurts of smoke bursting from their hands.

Tucson glanced down toward the adobe hut. Several of the Nirvan men were crowding at the doorway trying to take advantage of its walls. The door seemed to be locked. Then they scattered frantically trying to escape the fury of the onrushing cowpunchers. A few unleased shots in a final defiant stand.

Suddenly, Tucson realized the reason for the locked door in the adobe hut. Nirvan had retreated inside and was holding Louise Dixon as hostage. Tucson gave a loud yell. "I'll see you later, Lullaby. I always claimed Nirvan was my meat. Now I'm going to prove it."

Before Lullaby could join him, Tucson was dashing madly down the slope, the matched forty-fives that had belonged to Santone, gripped in both hands.

XXVIII

The thunder of the guns was deafening, as Tucson flashed down the slope. Powder smoke filled the air, and the heavy detonations of six-shooters were almost continual as the Wagon-Wheel men and their followers came within closer range. The outlaws had scattered wildly, some of them still shooting as they fled. Others were sprawled, groaning, on the earth. Two of them had managed to saddle up and were just mounting when Posthole Turner and his men closed in. There came a swift exchange of shots—and two empty saddles.

Tucson reached the adobe hut, hurled his weight against the closed door. It resisted his efforts. From within came the explosion of a six-shooter. A bullet splintered its way through the door, narrowly missing Tucson.

Tucson held his fire. Again and again he hurled his weight against the bolted door. It was commencing to give now. Once more, Nirvan's six-shooter roared. Tucson felt something hot burn through his body!

He drew off a few steps, then like a football player charging an opposing line, he leaped forward. The door sagged, then there came a rending crash as the bolt was torn loose from its fastening. The door slammed back against the inner wall.

The next instant, Tucson went plunging through the opening. Bullets were whining all around as he entered, but he was moving fast, providing a poor target. Both his guns came up, then he held his fire.

At the far end of the room stood Matt Nirvan, hiding behind the body of Louise Dixon. Nirvan clutched her about the waist with his left arm, while his right lifted his six-shooter toward Tucson. Tucson swore. It was impossible to fire at Nirvan without endangering the girl the man held before him as a shield.

A triumphant laugh burst from Nirvan's lips. "You haven't got a chance, Smith." Again he triggered a shot and Tucson staggered back as the leaden slug tore savagely into his body.

With an effort, Tucson righted himself, fighting to remain erect, Santone's matched six-shooters clutched in either hand, waiting for his chance.

Abruptly, Louise Dixon stooped over, leaving the upper half of Nirvan's body exposed. Tucson's right gun jumped, roaring, in his fist. He saw a tiny cloud of dust spurt from Nirvan's vest and knew he had scored a hit. A savage oath was torn from Nirvan's lips, as he was hurled back against the wall, losing his grip on the girl. Louise Dixon darted to one side, out of gun range.

Even as Nirvan righted himself and started to follow her, Tucson cut loose with both guns. Nirvan went to the floor, his right hand still pumping lead and flame.

Suddenly, Tucson found himself on the floor too. He braced himself on one hand, thumbed two swift shots. He saw Nirvan wince and sag back as the shots found their mark! Tucson fought to one knee, even as Nirvan raised his gun for a last desperate effort. Both men were nearly through now.

Only half knowing what he was doing, Tucson felt both guns kicking in his fists, the savage detonations shaking dust from the rafters overhead, as he released shot after shot. Nirvan sagged against the wall, eyes wide, jaw sagging. As he slid to the floor he pulled trigger with his dying strength.

Again, Tucson realized Nirvan hadn't missed. The shock of the bullet nearly hurled him flat, but he held himself upright. Through the drifting swirls of black powder smoke, he saw, as through a crimson haze, Nirvan's long form slide to the planking and lay without movement.

Blood was streaming into Tucson's eyes. One of Nirvan's bullets had ripped his scalp, but he was unconscious of feeling pain. It was only a feeling of dizziness that irritated him. He staggered nearer Nirvan's body, each step an effort. By now he had even forgotten that Louise

Dixon existed. His entire concentration was for Matt Nirvan. Now he stood wavering above the body of his enemy, his own consciousness fast slipping away.

A harsh laugh broke from Tucson's lips. "I always knew you were my meat, Nirvan. Now, I've proved it."

He slipped to one knee. Gripping his right gun tightly, he used the sight to cut a crimson X on Nirvan's forehead.

"Injun tactics," Tucson muttered thickly through the swelter of blood and sweat, "but that's something you deserve, Nirvan. . . ."

His words went uncompleted as he crashed down across Nirvan's lifeless body. He tried to struggle up, then suddenly his mind was swirled to nothingness in a deep black curtain of oblivion.

Tucson awoke slowly, opened his eyes and gazed blankly around. Next he realized he was in a bed, swathed in bandages. The morning sun was streaming in at an open window where lace curtains fluttered. It was a pleasant room, but Tucson had no memory of ever having seen it before. He wondered where he was and stirred slightly.

A voice penetrated his consciousness. "Oh, you're awake at last, Tucson."

He shifted his gaze and saw Louise Dixon standing over him. He smiled feebly into the girl's lovely features. "Yeah, I'm awake,"—

stretching a trifle then wincing at certain pains that shot through his body.

"You must lie still."

"That's all right with me," he agreed, relaxing. Things were coming clearer now. "That was one swell fight we had yesterday. If you hadn't been smart enough to stoop down that way—"

"Yesterday?" Louise laughed. "If you're referring to the day you shot Matt Nirvan, you're wrong. That was three weeks ago."

"Three weeks!" His eyes widened, jaw dropping.

Louise nodded. "It's been touch and go with you, Tucson. We were all worried for a time. Doctor Armstrong says the trip back nearly killed you, but we couldn't leave you down in Mexico. You're at the Wagon-Wheel, you know. You've been unconscious ever since that day—"

"I'll be blasted! How's Stony? Lullaby was wounded too—"

"They're both fine and anxious to see you. I'll call them, now that you've finally regained consciousness."

She went to the door and slipped out, leaving Stony and Lullaby to enter. Stony said, "You're on the mend at last, eh? Doc Armstrong said it wouldn't be much longer. But you need a heap of sleep to get back your strength. Louise has been nursing you right along—"

"I reckon we should shave him," Lullaby

drawled, grinning. "Look at that crop of whiskers!"

"You're not going to shave me anyway," Tucson smiled. "The only experience you ever had is shaving hogs—"

"Well?" Lullaby interrupted, chuckling.

Tucson laughed weakly. "It's good to hear you two handing out the old joshing. Lullaby, once I get some strength, I aim to rub your nose in the dirt for that crack. And then we can start roaming again—" He hesitated, looking at Stony. "Will you be with us?"

Stony flushed. "I'll be with you," he said sheepishly. "For a time there I had other ideas, but she—Louise—tells me she's been engaged a long time to a second cousin. Some jasper who attends a theological school in Indiany. It's just as well. Sometimes I think I've got too much itch in my feet to settle down permanent—" He broke off in some embarrassment.

"So we three will be hitting the trail soon," Tucson nodded, "as soon as they get a deputy to take my place."

"I've been attending to things in Manzanita," Lullaby said. "For all anybody knew I'd been appointed a deputy too. I haven't had any trouble. Things have been right peaceful. You knew you'd killed Nirvan, of course. The boys didn't take but two prisoners that day. Riker Wetzel lived long enough to confess to a long list of Nirvan's and his own crimes. Properties Nirvan stole through killing will be restored to dead men's heirs. So there's not a thing for you to fret about, Tucson."

Stony cut in, "Posthole and the other boys are waiting outside to see you, Tucson. Then you're supposed to go back to sleep."

"Fine, I'll see 'em," Tucson nodded drowsily, and promptly fell asleep again.

Center Point Large Print
600 Brooks Road / PO Box 1
Thorndike, ME 04986-0001 USA

(207) 568-3717

US & Canada:
1 800 929-9108
www.centerpointlargeprint.com